SIMON PACKHAM

Piccadilly

For Dimp

First published in Great Britain in 2014
by Piccadilly Press
A Templar/Bonnier publishing company
Deepdene Lodge, Deepdene Avenue, Dorking, Surrey, RH5 4AT
www.piccadillypress.co.uk

A catalogue record for this book is available
from the British Library

ISBN: 978 1 84812 384 7 (paperback)
ISBN: 978 1 84812 385 4 (ebook)

1 3 5 7 9 10 8 6 4 2

Printed in the UK by CPI Group (UK), Croydon, CR0 4TD

TRUST
GAMES

013997372 0

Simon Packham was born in Brighton. During his time as an actor he was a blind fiddler on HMS Bounty, a murderous vicar, a dodgy witness on The Bill and a variety of servants including Omar Sharif's personal footman and a coffin carrier for Dame Judi Dench.

He now writes fiction and lives in West Sussex with his wife, two children, and a cat called Pax.

Find out more at www.simonpackham.com and read an interview on www.piccadillypress.co.uk

Also available by Simon Packham:
Coming To Get You
The Bex Factor
Silenced
Firewallers

ACT ONE

Sweet Sixteen?

I'd almost convinced myself that the worst of it was over when Dad started winking at the waitress.

Grunt glanced up from his horseradish and blueberry ice cream, observing my twitching parent with post-ironic satisfaction and flashing me a 'pleasure in your pain' twinkle before I could escape back to my book.

'You'll never bag a boyfriend like that, Beth,' said Dad, aiming for light-hearted banter, but scoring at least 9.6 on the 'Irritate Your Daughter' scale.

'Like *what*?'

'All that reading. This is a Michelin-starred restaurant, not a public library. The least you can do is try and make polite conversation. Isn't that right, George?'

'Dunno really,' grunted Grunt, wiping his mouth on his Kraftwerk T-shirt.

I *could* have pointed out that *Le Grand Meaulnes* is one of the great coming of age novels (especially in its original French) or that I didn't want to go to his stupid fancy restaurant in the first place. But something was bugging me even more. 'What makes you think I want a boyfriend?'

'I don't know,' said Dad, still directing his middle-aged Tourette's symptoms at the short-skirted twenty-something working the espresso machine. 'There must be someone at school who's vaguely presentable.'

I *could* have pointed out that the testosterone-fuelled half of St Thomas's Community College was an acne-ravaged, technophile rabble with all the maturity of a tank of frogspawn. But four words covered it perfectly. 'You must be joking.'

Grunt pushed his bowl across the crisp white tablecloth and burped.

'How should I know anyway?' said Dad. 'I see so little of you these days.'

'Yes. And whose fault is that?'

'I have to work, Beth. You know that. What are a few days away each month if it means you can go to a decent university?'

It suited us both, and deep down I think we knew it. I mean, I loved my dad, but we hadn't exactly been hitting it off for the best part of half a decade. Now he was flying long haul, it meant having the house to myself sometimes – especially since I'd managed to persuade the lady from over the road that I was quite capable of preparing my own meals and she'd stopped 'popping in' every five minutes. It wasn't like I wanted to party all night or anything, but I could eat whatever I wanted, read a book without a lecture on the benefits of aerobic exercise or watch a movie with subtitles. What *he* got up to in LA or Barbados I wasn't sure, although from the way he was leering at that poor waitress, I had my suspicions.

'Will you *stop* doing that, please? You're just embarrassing yourself. You do realise how old she is.'

'What are you talking about?' said Dad. 'I was only . . .'

Albert Camus (the great thinker and one-time goalkeeper of the Algerian football team) once claimed that the only serious philosophical problem was suicide. I'd never quite understood what he meant, but it made perfect sense when I realised that Dad wasn't hitting on the waitress at all, and the full horror of the situation dawned on me.

Sadly, topping myself wasn't an option. The only alternative was to stare at the remains of my passion-fruit soufflé and wish my life away. How could Dad do this to me? And today, of all days.

'Happy birthday,' he said, as the flaming circle of Belgian chocolate humiliation glided inexorably towards me. The Sunday-night diners smiled sportingly, perhaps just a tiny bit grateful that it wasn't heading in their direction. Cheeks burning brighter than all sixteen candles (surely a discreet token would have been far more appropriate), my heart sank when Dad and the waitress launched into an auto-tuneless duet of 'Happy Birthday'.

'Nice,' said Grunt satirically. A moment later he was filming the tragic scene on his mobile, doubtless intending to tweet it to all twenty-six of his followers.

'Aren't you going to blow your candles out?' said Dad.

Personally, I can't think of anything more disgusting than spreading germs all over something you're about to eat. But I didn't want to disappoint the elderly couple by the window and, four puffs later, sixteen wisps of white smoke were drifting towards the ceiling.

Dad applauded, like I'd just won the Nobel Peace Prize. 'I can't believe my little girl is all grown up. It seems like only yesterday when —'

I grabbed a knife, desperate to stop him before he could make a speech. 'I'll cut it, shall I? Thanks, Dad, this is really . . .' I plunged the knife into the thick, gooey chocolate. 'How much do you want?'

For a while, it had the desired effect. Dad never reminisced with his mouth full, and if Grunt was pigging out ironically, it was his subtlest performance yet. In fact, the chances of making it through to the bill without further mishap looked fairly promising until Dad started groping under the table.

'Almost forgot,' he said, handing me a small package, trussed up in ribbon. 'I didn't really know what to get you, so I hope you like it.'

'I'm sure I will.' I tore suspiciously into the pink-ballooned wrapping paper and tried to sound like I meant it.

Dad nodded at the waitress, scrawling his signature in the air with an imaginary Biro. 'I got you a decent contract as well; two thousand minutes and unlimited data.'

'Thanks, Dad.'

'That is class,' said Grunt, who was shockingly sincere when it came to reclusive German synth combos or state-of-the-art gadgetry. 'Do you want me to set it up for you, Beth?'

'Yeah, thanks.'

'I can't believe how light it is. Makes *mine* look like an elephant.'

'Everyone wants one, apparently,' said Dad. 'The chap in the shop said they were queuing all the way to Starbucks the day it came out.'

Grunt almost wet himself when the screen lit up. 'The colours are so clear. And the wireless technology's amazing.'

'That's nice,' I said, willing the waitress to come across with the bill.

'I might as well update your contacts manually – shouldn't take too long,' said Grunt.

'How about a family photograph?' said Dad. 'Sorry, George, would you mind?'

'No problem,' said Grunt. 'Maybe later we could try panorama mode.'

Dad slid his chair towards mine and Grunt prepared

to immortalise us in eight glorious megapixels.

'Gorgonzola,' said Dad, like he always did when he had his photo taken.

I forced my features into an improbable grin.

'Let's have another one, shall we?' said Dad. 'Maybe Beth could smile this time.'

You probably hate me already. But if I sound like an ungrateful brat, let me at least talk you through the photograph and try to explain. It was almost four years since Mum died. I could just about cope with Christmas, but my birthday (Jan the second) brought on a creeping melancholy that never lifted until the first signs of spring. Hence the long face. I think Dad felt it too. Look carefully and you'd probably detect a sliver of sadness in his muddy grey eyes. Not that he ever talked about it. In fact I sometimes had this terrible feeling he was starting to forget.

So why all the fuss about an expensive new phone? Well for a start, I already had one in a drawer somewhere. No matter how sleek or packed with processing power, the latest smartphone seemed about as desirable as head lice. If that made me the sociopath they thought I was at school, fair enough. (Actually no one at St Thomas's had ever called me a sociopath; insults rarely rose above two syllables.) But what I hated most about Dad's presents was that they were such graphic reminders of how little he knew about me.

And what about the photographer? I'd known Grunt since . . . well, forever. Our mums took it in turns to meet us from Warmdene Infants. He was plain George Grant back then. It wasn't until Year Six that his reluctance to speak in fully formed sentences earned him his nickname. I suppose that suited me for a while, which is probably why it was the one friendship that survived. We still walked home together, and more often than not he'd pop back to my place and watch *Countdown* or mess about on the iPad Dad gave me. But something had changed. It was starting to feel – I don't know – awkward. He was talking more: sarcasm mainly, and feeble jokes that would have disgraced a Christmas cracker. That comment about updating my contacts (*shouldn't take too long*) had really hit home. If Grunt was my only friend, what did that say about me?

Does a thought like that creep up on you, or can everything change in the flash of a photograph? Whenever I look at that picture in the restaurant (I've often thought about deleting it but, for some reason, I just can't bring myself to) it certainly feels that way. Because that's when it hit me: if things were ever going to improve, *I* was the one that needed to change. Not totally reinvent myself, like some dumb Hollywood movie where the heroine starts dressing like a pole-dancer and hanging out with the local bad boy, but at least get a life that didn't look quite so pathetic.

I hadn't a clue how to go about it, of course. Unfortunately for me, the answer was just around the corner.

Out with
the In-crowd

'Oh God,' said Grunt, pulling down his *Wayne's World* cap. 'That's all we need.'

They were spilling onto the pavement outside Pizza Express: about fifteen of them, the girls hugging out mascara-stained farewells, the boys punching each other's shoulders and making animal noises, their warm breath mingling in the lamplight.

Grunt glanced anxiously over his shoulder for my dad. 'What are that lot doing here?'

All became clear when a bare-belly-buttoned Year Eleven, festooned in silly string and an outsized badge bearing the motto *Sixteen Today!*, tottered onto the pedestrianised cobbles in her six-inch heels wailing, 'I *love* you guys.'

''Ere AJ, give us a flash,' said a skinny-jeaned clone.

They all looked the same in their own clothes. But after they'd formed an amoeba-shaped cluster that bulged as far as the Cancer Shop, I soon realised we were in exalted company. If school was a popularity contest, then here were the winners: the boy who'd famously described Mr Catchpole as 'a sad, middle-aged loser' (to his *face*); all five members of the St Thomas's nu-ambient house band; the girl who set fire to the Design and Technology teacher's handbag; the twenty-four-hour party people; and a smattering of sports stars – not to mention the 'geniuses' who sprinkled the Learning Resources Centre with open sachets of tomato ketchup, and all-round school celebrity Duncan Fox. It was a glittering combination of the good, the bad, but *never* the ugly. Doubtless you'll be astonished to learn that Grunt and I weren't members of their ultra-exclusive coterie.

Neither was the boy in the leather jacket who stepped leeringly into the lamplight and barred our way. 'Look who it isn't,' he said. 'It's the prom queen and her bitch.'

Grunt reached instinctively for his most vulnerable body parts.

Dave Denyer was an 'in-crowd' wannabe. Now that Darren, his more illustrious cousin, was studying Advanced Thuggery (with Applied Menace) at the Sixth Form College, there was a possible opening for a trainee psychopath. 'Doing your bit for charity then, Beth?'

'Not sure what you mean, David,' I said.

He waved at the grubby mannequins in the Cancer

Shop window. 'Now we know where you get your clothes.'

Grunt's face unravelled with relief. The cavalry had arrived.

Dad smiled sheepishly and pulled on his gloves. 'Sorry about that. Damned things were under the table.' He surveyed the turbulent sea of youthful faces. 'Friends of yours, Beth?'

'Oh yeah,' smirked Dave Denyer. 'She's best mates with most of them, aren't you, Beth?'

Thanks to his faulty sarcasm detector, Dad looked pathetically pleased. It was unusual for him to be so insightful about his only daughter, but he'd somehow sussed out that I wasn't exactly spoilt for friends. Things were obviously looking up. 'Tell you what, why don't you and George stick around for a quick chat with your chums, while I pop back for the car.'

'It's okay, Dad, I —'

'I'll see you in a couple of minutes.'

Dave Denyer watched Dad disappear in the direction of the multi-storey before turning his attention to Grunt. 'Like your hat . . . *George*.'

Thirteen terms at St Thomas's had taught Grunt that resistance usually made things worse. 'Cheers, Dave.'

One or two of the in-crowd were taking a vague interest in the sideshow. It was all the encouragement Dave Denyer needed. 'Give us it here, then.'

Grunt's face betrayed no sign of emotion, but I knew for a fact he was working on a suitably cutting tweet.

Dave Denyer darted forward, liberating Grunt's cap with a triumphant, 'Yeeoohhh.' But when his crude, internet-virally-inspired victory dance failed to crack a smile, he moved on to something more sophisticated. 'Oh my God,' he said, sniffing the inside of Grunt's cap and pretending to puke. 'It's full of pus.'

I was furious that such puerile material was actually getting laughs. Even so, I should have known better. 'Just leave him alone, you . . . idiot.'

Dave Denyer Frisbeed Grunt's cap towards a distant rubbish bin and turned to face me with a gummy grin. 'What did you just call me?'

'Nothing,' I said, praying that Dad hadn't lost his car keys again. 'We're just going anyway.'

'Oh *please* don't go,' said Dave Denyer. 'You're the hottest girl in the whole school.'

(The biggest laugh of the night so far and a manly 'YOOOOerr.')

'I just wanna get to know you, babe.' He was right in my face, beckoning at me with his fat red tongue.

'I *said* we're going.'

Dave Denyer begged to differ. 'Not until you show us what you've got behind your back.'

In one hand was the box containing my new mobile, in the other my battered copy of *Le Grand Meaulnes*. He must have known instinctively which one I actually cared about, because two seconds later he was waving my prized paperback in the air. 'Le Grand *what*? Sounds disgusting – and it's not even in English.'

'It's a classic French novel,' I snapped, abandoning all hopes of a miraculous escape, 'by a guy called Alain-Fournier who died in the First World War.'

'So try telling someone who gives a toss,' said Dave Denyer, selecting a random page and 'reading' aloud in a fake French accent. 'Ma name eez Beth. I zink a am – 'ow you say – zee dogz berllox? Burt a em murch too stupeed to —'

I flailed desperately at *Le Grand Meaulnes*, grabbing only a handful of cold air as he whisked it above my head. 'Just give it to me.'

'Any time, darling,' said Dave Denyer. 'All you got to do is say the word.'

And then Grunt, who'd finally retrieved his *Wayne's World* cap, said something really stupid. In fact, it was so out of character I could hardly believe it. 'You heard her,' he said. 'Give it back.'

Dave Denyer had a real weakness for old-school clichés. 'Gonna make me?'

Perhaps they were enjoying it in a cool, ironic way, because the crowd was rearranging itself into a semi-circle. Even Duncan Fox had broken off from the girl who organised the fashion show to get a better view.

It was the mismatch of the New Millennium. Dave Denyer looked capable of holding his own in any number of futuristic killing scenarios. Grunt, on the other hand, was a pizza-loving Munchkin whose only experience of hand-to-hand combat was on his laptop. Even so, it didn't stop him charging at the Frenchliterature-wielding thug. 'I *SAID*, GIVE IT BACK.'

'What's the matter – past your bedtime?'

It was all a bit retro for Year Eleven, but Denyer's audience seemed to be warming to it. 'Watch out, Dave,' said Duncan Fox. 'He's got a bun in his pocket.'

Two seconds later, Grunt was in a headlock. Dave Denyer forced him into the gutter, like a lion downing an antelope. 'Big mistake . . . *George*.'

He might have been a total lunatic, but Grunt was kind of like a (slightly annoying) brother to me. What else was I supposed to do? 'That's enough,' I said, sounding about as convincing as that Design and Technology teacher who was always off with stress. 'Just leave him alone, okay?'

'Thought you'd be pleased,' said Dave Denyer. 'I'm going to give your chubster boyfriend a French lesson.'

'What do you . . .?'

Grunt groaned as a timeless French classic began beating him about the head.

The prospect of a happy ending looked doubtful – just like the novel. Dave Denyer was warming up for the big finish. All I could think of was to grab him round the neck and start pulling.

But he seemed quite pleased about it. 'Brilliant,' he said, brushing me off like a collection of toenail clippings. 'Now I get to kill two birds with one book.' (*Two birds with one tome* would have been better, but I wasn't going to write his jokes for him.)

Whatever hilarious form of humiliation Dave Denyer

had up his blue-checked sleeve, I knew I wasn't going to like it. So I closed my eyes and tried to remember the French word for pomegranate.

But then a miracle happened.

A voice from the in-crowd cut above the expectant buzz of audience participation. I recognised it instantly. The last time I'd heard it, it was trying to sell me heroin.

'Oi Denyer, stop being a dick.'

Dave Denyer recognised it too, dropping his weapon and turning to face his critic with a half-hearted snarl. 'I was just defending myself. What do you expect?'

'Get off on it, do you,' said the voice, 'persecuting women?'

'She called me an idiot.'

'Yeah, and she was right,' said the voice. 'You're just jealous because she's so much smarter than you.'

'And that's not difficult,' said Duncan Fox, who hadn't become a major school celebrity by not knowing when to change sides.

It was the kind of voice that everyone listened to: clear and confident, but with the hint of a sexy growl. 'You're such a kid, aren't you? I can't believe you think you're funny. Why don't you go home? No one wants you here anyway.'

Dave Denyer rose from his human footstool. His audience had already turned their fickle backs on him. 'Yeah, well, I was going anyway,' he said, nodding at the keyboards player from Neologism and trying to make a dignified exit.

'You all right, Beth?' said the voice, softer now, and friendlier too.

I knew her name, of course, but I was surprised she remembered mine. Hannah Taylor was in my GCSE Drama group. We'd worked together on the assessed improvisation about the drug dealer. Even so, I don't think we'd exchanged more than a couple of sentences.

'I'm fine thanks,' I said.

'Talk about immature,' said Hannah. 'Like most of the kids at school.' Grunt was sniffing his *Wayne's World* cap. 'How's your boyfriend anyway?'

'Looks okay to me. Only he's not my boyfriend,' I added hastily.

Hannah smiled. 'Probably for the best.'

I wanted to thank her. The trouble was, every sentence I planned in my head sounded either way too sycophantic or the words of a timid four-year-old. It's hard to explain. Meeting her in the street was kind of like running into a movie star. She was the sort of person who made the whole school thing look like the happiest days of her life, not the grim survival exercise most of us knew it to be. Top of every guest list, the first person you'd vote for in a school election if it wasn't a St Thomas's tradition to elect the joke candidate, and a dead cert for the front page of *The County Times* on results day, Hannah Taylor was the complete package. She was clever, but not the kind of clever that got you excommunicated for knowing words like sycophantic – in three languages. She looked good too, but without

17

being so drop-dead gorgeous that everyone hated her.

But it was more than that. Hannah always seemed older than the rest of us. I'm not just talking about her period-drama cleavage – that was enviable, especially to someone as flat-chested as me – but she had a maturity about her that I coveted even more. She treated the St Thomas's staff more like equals than academic prison warders, and rumour had it that when the DT teacher threatened to kill herself, it was Hannah who walked her round the school field until she calmed down.

No wonder I was tongue-tied. 'I, er . . .'

'Is that what I think it is?' she said, pointing excitedly at my new phone.

'Yeah.'

'You are *so* lucky. I'd give my texting hand for one of them!'

Up until that moment, it was going straight in the drawer with the other one. From now on, it was definitely accompanying me to school. 'It's a birthday present from my dad.'

'Is it your birthday then?'

'Uh huh.'

Hannah glanced meaningfully at Grunt. 'That's really sad.'

I had to agree with her.

'Anyway, got to go,' she said. 'School again tomorrow – I hate the first day of term.'

'Yeah . . . right . . . Hey, Hannah, I just wanted to —'

But it was too late – she'd gone. And with typically

brilliant timing, Dad rounded the corner, smiling apologetically. 'No change for the car park I'm afraid. You don't have a spare pound coin do you, George?'

Grunt nodded.

It was the voice again. 'Sorry, Beth, I think you forgot this.' Hannah handed me my dog-eared paperback. 'Is it any good?'

'Yes, really good,' I said, trying to sound like a normal person and not a critic. 'I think you might enjoy it.'

Dad seemed keen to get in on the act. 'Hello, there. I'm Beth's dad.'

'Hello, Beth's dad,' said Hannah. 'Love the new phone by the way. She's so lucky to have a dad like you.'

I could have sworn I saw Dad blush.

'You're the pilot, right?' said Hannah.

'How did you know that?'

'Beth mentioned it when she was a drugs mule.'

'What do you . . .?'

'In Drama,' smiled Hannah. 'We're both in the same group.'

Dad laughed. 'Which way are you headed? We could give you a lift if you like.'

'No, you're all right,' said Hannah. 'I'm walking with Candice and AJ. It was nice to meet you though.'

Grunt was sulking in the back seat, metaphorically licking his wounds.

Dad on the other hand was disgustingly chirpy. 'She seemed very . . . pleasant. Who was she, by the way?'

That's what I mean about the flash of a camera. Half an hour before it would have seemed impossible; one glimpse of Grunt in the rear-view mirror told me it was just what I needed. She knew my name. That was a start. And why would she have bothered to step in like that if she didn't like me?

It was far-fetched, to say the least. So why was I so sure I could make it happen? In fact, I was already road-testing the words in the back of my head – and they sounded good. Once they were out in the open, there was no going back.

'That was my new friend . . . Hannah,' I said.

Morning After
the Night Before

The next time I saw Hannah was at the end of first break.
I followed her into the reception block toilets and made
a feeble attempt to start a conversation.

'Hi Hannah.'

She was retouching her eye-liner. 'Oh . . . hi.'

My cheeks were already aching from smiling too
hard. 'Doing your make-up, are you?'

'Yeah,' said Hannah. 'I don't know what happened in
History, but I look a right mess.'

'You look fine,' I said, pretending to study my split
ends in the mirror. 'I'm the one who should be worried.
My hair's a nightmare.'

'Have you tried Bed Head?' said Hannah. 'It's
amazing.'

'Right . . . thanks . . . sounds good. I'll give it a go.'

I'd rehearsed the next bit in my head. It was supposed to sound 'quirky and interesting', but when I heard it out loud it was more like borderline weird. 'Did you know that according to an ancient Chinese proverb, if you save someone's life you become responsible for them forever?'

'Oh . . . right.'

'But don't worry. I won't hold you to it.'

'Sorry,' said Hannah. 'I don't quite . . .'

'I'm talking about last night. Outside Pizza Express? You saved my life – well, metaphorically anyway.'

'No problem,' said Hannah. 'Dave Denyer's a right idiot.'

Movies and novels are full of improbable friendships. Donkeys and ogres, fairies and boys who refuse to grow up (plenty of *them* at St Thomas's), little old ladies and Death Row serial killers – so why shouldn't I be friends with Hannah Taylor? Last night it had seemed so easy. But in the cold light of the reception block toilets, I was struggling to string a couple of sentences together. That wasn't my only problem. Hannah had a whole army of friends already. What would she want a new one for?

And as if to illustrate the point perfectly, the cubicle door swung open and out slunk AJ. Several bucketfuls of foundation had failed to conceal her attractive shade of green. 'God I feel rough.'

'Told you to take it easy, didn't I?' said Hannah.

'Yeah, thanks Mum,' said AJ. She turned to me with a headachey scowl. 'Well that was really really interesting. If there's one thing I love, it's a Chinese proverb. What are you talking to her for anyway?'

'I'll talk to whoever I want, thank you,' said Hannah. 'But if you're *really really* interested, we were comparing notes on last night. Did you know it was Beth's birthday too?'

AJ raised a savagely plucked eyebrow. 'Well thank God I don't believe in astrology. Because I'd hate to think I had anything in common with *her*.'

Hannah flashed me an apologetic smile. 'I think I'd better get moving. I've got Catchpole next. He'll go mental if I'm late again.'

'Oh right,' I said, holding the door for them. 'I'll see you in Drama then.'

'Yeah, great,' said Hannah. 'Forgot it was Drama.'

'We should be starting our devised performance pieces. Maybe we could work together.'

'She's working with me, aren't you babe?' said AJ, grabbing Hannah's arm and guiding her to the door.

I stood and watched as they walked arm in arm down the corridor, mortified at AJ's final cackling comment before they disappeared into the crowd: 'Just wait till I tell Candice about your little stalker.'

Trust
Games

'Where's Carver then?' whispered Duncan Fox. '*She's* the one with the timekeeping fetish.'

It was true. Miss Carver was fanatical about punctuality. According to her, the first rule of the theatre was, 'It's not fair and don't be late.'

'Probably shaving,' said AJ, doodling a flower on her Drama folder.

No one noticed him at first. He stepped out from behind the black drapes that lined the drama studio walls and coughed. But his skinny black jeans, slim-fit black shirt and designer frames acted as a kind of camouflage. He looked more like a fashion-conscious lab assistant than a proper teacher.

'Sorry, mate,' said Duncan Fox. 'Do you know where Miss Carver is?'

'At home with her feet up, I hope,' said the man in black.

'What do you mean?'

'She's on maternity leave. Didn't she say anything before Christmas?'

'I knew she was getting fat,' said AJ. 'Thought it was all the doughnuts.'

Hannah smiled sympathetically. 'You look lost. Where do you want to get to?'

'I'm Mr Moore,' he said, in a voice almost as soft as the downy hairs on his chin. 'I'll be covering for Miss Carver until next term.'

I remember feeling disappointed. He might have been more photogenic than his predecessor, but at least with Miss Carver I could be sure of a decent grade. It can't have been that long since our new Drama teacher was taking exams himself.

'Hey sir,' said AJ.

'Yes.'

'You look really young, sir. Are you experienced?'

Much laughter as Mr Moore twisted his thin black tie around his thin white fingers. 'What?'

AJ twisted the knife. 'Have you *done* it before, sir . . . teaching I mean?'

Hannah glared at her so-called friend. 'Don't listen to AJ, sir. She's always like this when she's coming on.'

An even bigger laugh. AJ slashed her imaginary claws at Hannah.

'Right, that's enough,' said Mr Moore. 'Let's have

some quiet please.'

A high-pitched *Oooo-er* followed by an uneasy silence.

'Now I know you'll be working on your devised pieces for the summer, but I think one of you wants to submit an original movie script as well.'

My cheeks sizzled. 'That's me, sir. Beth Bridges.'

'What's it called,' said Candice Barrett, '*Last Train to Loserville?*'

Mr Moore ripped off his designer frames, eyeballing Candice and her sniggering audience. Clark Kent suddenly became Superman. 'Okay, let's stop right there, shall we? Now I don't want to say this again, so listen carefully. The drama studio is a place where everyone should feel safe. Somewhere you're not afraid to take risks and make mistakes. What I will not tolerate is any of this schoolgirl bitchiness crap. Do I make myself clear?'

'Yeah,' mumbled Candice.

Never mind global warming, Mr Moore's smile would have melted the ice-caps. 'So, with that in mind, after we've all introduced ourselves, I think we'll start with a couple of trust games.'

Groans all round. They preferred libellous improvisations featuring members of staff or Simpsons characters behaving weirdly.

Grunt had his hand up. 'I'm doing Lighting and Sound Design, sir. Shall I go and check the mixing board?'

'Not today,' said Mr Moore. 'I think it would be more useful if you joined us.'

There was general amusement at the thought of Grunt acting. Why he'd opted for Drama in the first place was a mystery.

'Okay guys, let's pull these chairs back and get into a circle.' He'd obviously won some hearts and minds with his stance on schoolgirl bitchiness, because we cleared the space in a new world record.

'Now I want to get to know you all as quickly as possible. So for my benefit, I'd like you to shout out your names and perform a signature gesture. For instance: Steve Moore!' He jumped in the air, clicking his heels together, like the Artful Dodger in last year's school play. 'We'll start with the guy with the messenger bag and work our way round the circle.'

Perhaps once he'd got to know us better, Mr Moore would have started with a different trust game. Pairing Candice with Duncan Fox and instructing them to lead each other blindfolded round the drama studio was a recipe for disaster.

So no one was very surprised when a high-pitched scream brought the game to a premature conclusion and all the followers ripped off their school ties to see what had happened.

'That's disgusting. How could you *do* that?'

'I never touched him,' said Candice. 'What do you think I am?'

'I *know* what you are,' said Duncan. 'You're a complete —'

'FOR GOD'S SAKE SHUT UP.'

27

The whole drama studio went quiet. Because it wasn't the angry voice we were expecting; this time it was Hannah.

'Why do you have to mess about the whole time? I'm trying to learn something here. Can't you just give it a rest?'

I knew Hannah loved Drama, but it was probably the first time that I realised how much. It was good to know we had *something* in common.

'Yes, thank you . . . Hannah,' said Mr Moore, who'd been watching intently from the sidelines. 'I think I'll take it from here. Now before we get on to some coursework, I want to try one last "classic" trust game.'

'You've got to be joking,' said AJ. 'No offence, but why would you trust anyone in this school?'

'It's important if you're going to be working together,' said Mr Moore. 'Look, I'll show you if you like. Anyone brave enough to give me a hand?'

Hannah was first to raise hers.

'No, no – let's try someone else, shall we?' A forest of feminine index fingers reached for the sky. Mr Moore tried to see the funny side. 'What's the matter, boys, don't you trust me?'

'We don't even know you,' said a gruff voice at the back.

'All right then,' said Mr Moore. 'Looks like I'll have to choose someone myself.'

The last time I'd seen such unbridled enthusiasm was at a 'gifted and talented' Maths workshop in Year Seven.

'Sir, sir, sir . . . sir!'

'How about you?' said Mr Moore. 'The girl who's writing the movie script. It's Beth, isn't it?'

There were more than a few jealous mutterings as I stepped towards him, my second blush of the lesson spreading like wildfire. 'That's right, sir. Beth Bridges.'

'Okay, Beth, I want you to stand with your back to me. Don't worry, I'm right behind you.'

His aftershave was woody and understated; nothing like the evil stuff St Thomas's boys doused themselves in.

'Now, fold your arms across your chest – that's right, like you're in a straitjacket.'

There were a few giggles, but most seemed keen to see what would happen next.

'Now, in your own time, Beth; all you have to do is close your eyes and let yourself go.'

I could feel the others willing him to drop me. But his voice was calm and reassuring, hypnotic almost. Maybe AJ was right; maybe there weren't many people you could trust at St Thomas's. But I had a feeling that Mr Moore was one of them.

So I closed my eyes and fell back into his arms.

Before the bell went, Mr Moore made an 'important' announcement. 'I just want to remind you all about the end of term production.'

There were a few sarcastic *Ooohs*, like the sound they made when someone won a rubbish prize in a school raffle.

'Auditions are next week. They're open to everyone of course, but it would be great to have some of you guys on board. There's a sign-up sheet on the door.'

'What's it going to be anyway?' said Candice Barrett.

'*Romeo and Juliet*,' said Mr Moore, almost as if he was expecting a standing ovation. 'I'll be directing and Miss Hoolyhan's going to help with the music.'

'Fancy her do you, sir?' came the inevitable response.

But Duncan Fox was looking seriously underwhelmed. 'Miss Carver said we were doing *Rent*. It's a musical about an exotic dancer with AIDS.'

'Yes, well, Mr Edmonds wasn't sure it was quite right for St Thomas's. He thought it might be a good idea if we tackled some Shakespeare.'

'But why?' said Duncan Fox. '*Oliver!* was excellent, and that kid who died in the car crash was dead funny in *Little Shop of Horrors*.'

'Well I think it sounds all right,' said Hannah. 'You can put my name down for a start.'

'I like the scene in the swimming pool,' said Candice Barrett. 'The rest of it's a bit crap though.'

'No swimming pools I'm afraid,' said Mr Moore. 'This is the original stage version.'

'But his plays are well boring,' said AJ. 'They go on forever, and they're about a million years old.'

Mr Moore seemed to come alive, like Frankenstein's monster at a book club. 'About four hundred years, actually; that's what's amazing about them. The themes are so contemporary. Take *Romeo and Juliet* for instance.

There's the transforming power of love, gang culture, the conflict between love and duty. And the language is incredibly rich. Did you know that Shakespeare invented more than a thousand new words and sayings that are still in use today? Auspicious, castigate . . . fool's paradise . . .' He allowed us a few seconds to be suitably impressed. 'So come on guys, who else thinks they might be up for it?'

Every girl apart from Candice and AJ had her hand up.

'Brilliant,' said Mr Moore. 'But how about some of you boys as well?'

'Yeah, all right,' said Duncan Fox. 'Miss Carver had already promised me Roger, but I suppose you'll need a Romeo.'

He was so predictable. Everyone knew he fancied the pants off Hannah.

But the next volunteer came as more of a surprise. I knew we needed more boys, but I couldn't help feeling slightly irritated when Grunt stuck his hand up. 'I could help with the lights if you like.'

'Good man,' said Mr Moore, who was obviously a lot happier about it than I was. 'Now if you're planning on auditioning, read the play over the weekend and try to decide which part you might be right for. And don't forget that sign-up sheet.'

'I thought you got stage fright,' said Grunt, as I printed my name under Duncan Fox's. 'Remember the time you puked on that innkeeper?'

'Yeah, I was, like, five years old.'

Grunt was right. The thought of learning all that poetry and then saying it in front of an audience of drowsy parents and their hyper-critical offspring had already coated my palms with a layer of sweat. But I really wanted to try acting again, and Mr Moore seemed like the perfect director. He was kind and sensitive and you could see how passionate he was about Shakespeare.

Plus which, there were bound to be lunchtime rehearsals, maybe a couple of evenings after school – perhaps even a session or two on the weekends. With Candice and AJ out of the picture, it was the perfect opportunity to get to know Hannah.

ACT TWO

An Actor Prepares

The day before the auditions, I asked Grunt to work on a scene with me. He wasn't exactly my idea of a dream co-star, but Dad was still in LA, so I popped the question the moment we got back from school.

'You're not serious, are you?'

It was just the confidence boost I needed. 'Why shouldn't I be? Look, are you going to help me or not?'

'I'll do it if I can order pizza,' said Grunt, grabbing my iPad from the coffee table and settling into his well-worn groove on the sofa.

'Fine,' I said, surprised he'd agreed so easily. He hated reading out loud. Mrs Woolf had stopped asking him after the *Pride and Prejudice* incident in Year Nine.

'Give us your debit card then.'

I slipped it off the mantelpiece and handed it over.

'Surprised you don't know the number by now.'

'Ha, ha.'

Grunt was probably the most contented person I knew, but he'd always been jealous of my debit card. Dad gave it to me when he started flying long haul again. It made him feel less guilty about leaving me 'home alone'. Every month he put more money into my account. But I hardly ever used it, and Grunt was always encouraging me to 'splash the cash'. 'Get some dough balls as well if you like.'

'Cheers,' said Grunt, bringing up the website and plumping predictably for his beloved Meat Feast. 'Do you want anything?'

I was already sick with pre-audition nerves. 'I'll fix myself a snack later.'

'Pizza'll be here in fifteen minutes,' said Grunt. 'Let's get this over with, shall we?'

I'd printed it out the night before. 'It's the scene where Romeo first meets Juliet at the masked ball.'

Grunt studied the sheet of paper, wrinkling his nose and sniffing dubiously. 'Are you sure about this?'

'What do you mean?'

'These are, like, the two main characters, aren't they? Weren't you supposed to pick a part you'd be right for?'

'Are you saying I couldn't be Juliet?'

'Well no . . . you could be,' said Grunt. 'I just hope Mr Whatshisface sees you that way.'

'Mr Moore.'

'Yeah . . . whatever.'

35

It's not like I hadn't thought about it. I doubt anyone would pick me out of a police line-up as a natural Juliet, but the more times I'd read the play, the more I'd fallen in love with her. And if I was going to audition, I might as well try out for the leading part. 'Well come on then, stand up.'

'Do I have to?'

'If you want pizza, you do.'

Grunt rose reluctantly, turning to face me with one hand in his pocket and a look of boredom marinated in fear. 'What do we do now?'

'Just stay in the moment,' I said, recycling the first acting cliché I could think of. 'You're the one who speaks first.'

He sounded like Steven Hawking after a software malfunction. '*My . . . lips two blushing pilgrims, ready stand to . . . smooth that rough touch with a . . . kiss.*'

'*Good pilgrim, you do wrong your hand to —*'

'Hang on a minute,' said Grunt. 'Have you actually learned this stuff?'

'Got a problem with that?'

'No, no it's good,' he said, toeing the floor like a counting horse. 'I mean . . . *you're* good. In fact, I think you're —'

'Look, could you keep still please? It's really putting me off.'

'Fine.'

'Right, let's get on with it, shall we? *For saints have hands that pilgrims' hands do touch, and palm to palm is*

36

holy palmers' kiss.'

Grunt practically jumped out of his skin when I reached across for his hand. 'What are you doing?'

'*Palm to palm.* They're supposed to be touching hands. It says so in the script.'

'Oh . . . right,' murmured Grunt, placing his sweaty hand against mine and swallowing hard. '*Have not saints lips and holy palmers too?*'

'*Ay, pilgrim, lips that must be used in prayer.*'

He seemed even shorter than usual. Maybe that's why he couldn't look me in the eye. 'What's it all mean anyway?'

'Don't you get it? In a minute they're going to kiss.'

Grunt snatched his hand back. 'I'm not sure if . . .'

'Don't be stupid, it's only *me*. Look, we're not actually going to —'

'I need the toilet,' he said, grabbing my iPad and heading for the door.

'Don't take it in there with you. It's not hyge—'

Too late: Romeo had already left the stage. I flopped back on the sofa and gave myself a mental pep talk. At least I hadn't forgotten my lines, and if I could act with a block of wood like Grunt, I could act with anyone.

Five minutes later, he reappeared with my iPad. 'You'll never guess what I've found.'

'Not another stupid dance craze?'

'Better than that,' he said, sitting down beside me and pressing play. 'Take a look.'

'Oh my God, it's . . .'

'Yeah,' said Grunt, looking a lot more relaxed now he was back in sarcasm mode. 'That man is such an idiot. He was walking down the corridor the other day in a crap pair of headphones.'

I couldn't believe what I was seeing. It was Mr Moore – or 'Steve Moore, performance poet' to give him his full title. He was standing in front of a black curtain dressed in ripped jeans and a polo shirt. Perhaps it was because he was a teacher, but I fully expected the two hundred and forty-ninth play of his poem 'Grown Up' to be a disaster (especially as comments had been disabled). So I was totally gobsmacked when he grabbed the microphone, and started prowling the stage in his well-worn Converses.

'Okay,' he said. 'This is a poem about growing up.

'When I was only seven,
My mother said to me,
Let's talk about the future,
And what you want to be.
A butcher or an astronaut?
A critic or a spy?
A poet or a plumber?
But this was my reply:

' *"I wanna be a grown-up,*
I wanna have my say,
I wanna stay up very late and watch Match of the Day.
I wanna be an adult,

I want it really bad,
I wanna have a bank account
And learn to swear like Dad.
I wanna be a grown-up,
I wanna be a man,
Can't stay a kid forever,
So !!** you Peter Pan."

'And now I'm twenty-seven,
I'll tell you who's to blame,
A mum who never told me,
That growing up was lame.
 A world of pain and pensions,
Of nightmares made from dreams,
Where Peter Pan drives a Transit Van,
And no one hears you scream:

'"Don't wanna be a grown-up,
Don't wanna have my say,
The clowns and politicians,
Don't listen anyway.
Don't wanna be an adult,
Don't wanna grow at all,
Don't want the gas-billed future,
The pram against the wall.
Don't wanna be a grown-up,
Don't want to act mature,
If that's the way I'm headed,
I wanna find the cure."'

The audience at the 'UK Poetry Slam' whooped politely, like trainee Americans. Mr Moore acknowledged them with a casual 'Thankyouverymuch' and jumped down off the stage.

'What a loser, eh?' said Grunt.

But I didn't think so. He seemed so confident and in control, not to mention pretty cute in his little black polo shirt.

Was it wrong to feel that way about a teacher?

Next

According to Mr Moore 'biting your thumb' at someone (jerking your thumbnail forward over your front teeth) was the Elizabethan equivalent of St Thomas's favourite obscene gesture, so we finished the warm-up running round the drama studio trading Shakespearian insults.

'Do you bite your thumb at us, sir?'
'I do bite my thumb, sir.'

'Do you bite your thumb at us, sir?'
'I do bite my thumb, sir.'

'Do you bite your thumb at us, sir?'
'I do bite my thumb, sir.'

'DO YOU BITE YOUR THUMB AT US, SIR?'
'I DO BITE MY THUMB, SIR!'

'Okay . . . Okay,' shouted Mr Moore. 'I think we'd better move on. But that's some really good work there. Let's get the chairs into a semi-circle and then we can hear you read.'

It said on the internet that a couple of deep breaths could calm the nerves. All I felt was dizzy and on the verge of chucking up my pannini. I'd assumed the actual audition bit would be in private, but Mr Moore and Miss Hoolyhan wanted us to watch each other and show our support.

The ones going for the smaller parts were up first, taking it in turns to mangle a few lines from the prologue:

'Two households, both alike in . . . dignity . . . in fair . . . Ve . . . ro . . . na . . .'

Mr Moore and Miss Hoolyhan scribbled copious notes and offered words of encouragement. 'That's terrific, Toby. Now try saying it like you mean it.'

Things got better when we moved onto the leading roles. A girl called Magda made a pretty good stab at Lady Montague and Pete Hughes, that loathsome Year Ten show-off and wannabe hair model, was a shoe-in for Mercutio.

'Right,' said Mr Moore, flicking through his reporter's notebook, 'it's time to have a look at our star-crossed lovers. I've got three of each here, so we'll pair you up randomly and try the part where Romeo first spots Juliet. Let's start with Holly and Amir.'

I couldn't believe my luck. I'd actually learned the

whole scene. And it probably didn't hurt that Holly and Amir were totally crap. But my heart started doing aerobics again when Mr Moore put them out of their misery. 'Thank you, that was . . . really interesting. Now who's next? Ah yes, Duncan and Hannah. Let's take it from the same place, shall we?'

I'd been so paralysed with nerves that I hadn't really given it much thought. But it was obvious. Hannah was pretty much perfect for Juliet. And Duncan Fox had probably written his own programme notes already. He winked at his Year Nine fan club and swaggered up to Juliet.

'*If I profane with this unworthiest hand . . .*'

I didn't know how to feel about Hannah. I wanted her to do well, but I'd secretly set my heart on Juliet. So when she stumbled over her lines, I couldn't help feeling slightly pleased – and then a bit mean for having felt that way.

'*Good pilgrim you do wrong your hand too much. Which man . . . which man . . .* sorry . . . I don't know . . .'

'It's *mannerly*,' said Mr Moore. 'Now keep going, you're doing great.'

Hannah smiled and flicked a strand of long, chestnutty hair from her face. 'Cheers, sir. *Which mannerly devotion shows in this . . .*'

She was fine after that. And they looked depressingly good together. There was a definite on-stage chemistry, which I had a feeling could easily work its way backstage too. Hannah was gazing into his eyes, like she really meant it.

The first time they kissed it was a peck on the cheek. *'Give me my sin again.'*

The next time they really went for it. Duncan Fox might have kissed her first, but if Hannah was only faking, she was a brilliant actress. The audience offered a running commentary as they locked mouths like a pair of passionate toilet plungers.

'Get a room!'

'Eeeyagggh . . . gross.'

'Way to go, Dunc!'

And the Year Sevens giggled on.

In the end, Mr Moore practically had to pull them apart. 'Right, thank you . . . we'll leave it there I think. That was very . . .' He searched for the right word, but didn't find it. 'So, who's next?'

Miss Hoolyhan was fiddling distractedly with her charm bracelet. 'Our last couple are Beth and Marlon.'

Marlon was the boy in Year Eight with a permanent cold. We stared at each other for half an eternity, until at last he ran his finger down the crumpled piece of paper with his lines on and opened his mouth to speak. Nothing came out, just a bead of snot peering from his stage left nostril. But my fading hopes of theatrical immortality were shattered completely when Marlon finally managed to mutter, 'I can't.'

'It's all right,' said Miss Hoolyhan, glaring at the cruel souls who thought it was funny (practically everyone) and leading him back to his seat. 'Don't worry, Marlon, we're turning the Chorus into a 1960s skiffle group, so I'll be looking for some actor/musicians.'

'What do you want *me* to do?' I said. 'Shall I sit down?'

'Stay right there,' said Mr Moore, jumping out of his seat with the script in his hands. 'I'll read with you, if you like.'

I *did* like.

Miss Hoolyhan reached for the rash on the inside of her elbow. 'Do you think that's a good i—?'

'It's fine,' said Mr Moore, smiling encouragingly and finding the place in his *Penguin Shakespeare*. 'I'm sure I can manage to watch Beth's performance at the same time. Let's go for it, shall we?'

His aftershave was like a sedative, and his voice so relaxing my nerves seemed to vanish. I didn't even care about the hecklers.

'*If I profane with my unworthiest hand . . .*'

Mr Moore made the verse come alive, and unlike Marlon he didn't make you feel like you wanted to run a mile in the opposite direction. Far from it in fact, because by the end of the scene I was so in character that I'd almost forgotten he was a teacher. And just for a nanosecond, I had this silly idea that he was actually going to kiss me. I mean I knew he wouldn't, but when the moment came I closed my eyes and waited, just in case. Nothing happened, of course. And I'm sure no one noticed that I was a fraction late with my next line. '*You kiss by the book.*'

'Careful, sir,' said Marlon, who seemed to have miraculously rediscovered the power of speech. 'You'll get arrested.'

'Okay, Beth, I think we'll leave it there,' said Mr Moore, his face reddening slightly before recovering its customary equilibrium. 'Thanks guys, that was excellent. You've given us a lot to think about, haven't they, Fleur?'

'Yes, *Mr Moore*,' said Miss Hoolyhan, pretending to be all professional, but clearly loving the fact that he'd used her Christian name. 'Okay you lot, we need to pop out to the office for a quick chat.'

'That's right,' said Mr Moore. 'I don't believe in prolonging the agony, so give us ten minutes and we'll get back to you with our decisions.'

'Don't do anything I wouldn't do, miss,' called a voice from the audience, as they exited stage right to ironic applause.

The good behaviour lasted about five minutes until a red-headed Year Ten put her iPod in the speaker dock and started blasting out that song they played to death last summer. Pete Hughes, who'd finally finished grooming himself, climbed onto a table, swaying rhythmically, while the others filmed it on their phones. Suddenly, everyone in the drama studio was gyrating to that underwater-swimming dance, which had only just infected the internet.

And the place was really pumping when the door swung open and in steamed a middle-aged PSHE teacher with a Tesco bag. 'What the hell is going on in here?'

If anything, the eerie silence was more sudden than the cacophony.

Pete Hughes jumped down from the table. '*Romeo and Juliet* auditions, sir.'

'Get your thumb out of your mouth, boy. I can't hear a word you're saying. Now who's supposed to be in charge?'

'Mr Moore, sir,' said Pete Hughes. 'The new Drama teacher.'

'And how long have you been left unsupervised?'

Once again, it was Hannah who sprang to the rescue. She was a far better liar than I could ever be. 'They've only been gone a second, sir. Miss Hoolyhan got something in her eye, so Mr Moore took her to his office to find the first aid kit. I'm sure they'll be back soon.'

They appeared right on cue, Mr Moore grinning nervously at the authority figure in the 'vintage' 1990s suit. 'Hi there, don't think we've met. I'm Steve, Steve Moore, acting head of Drama.'

'Colin Catchpole, acting director of Student Welfare.'

'Sorry about the noise,' said Miss Hoolyhan. 'We were only —'

'Don't worry, Miss Hoolyhan,' said Mr Catchpole, lingering dreamily over her Celtic surname. 'Hannah here explained what happened.' He turned less affably to Mr Moore. 'Word to the wise, Steven; you can't leave this rabble on their own, not for a second.'

'Yes of course,' said Mr Moore. 'It won't happen again.'

'I'll leave you to it then,' said Mr Catchpole, turning to his favourite Music teacher with a gap-toothed smile.

'Goodnight . . . Fleur. I do hope that eye of yours clears up.'

'Thank you,' said Miss Hoolyhan, squinting thoughtfully as the acting director of Student Welfare took his leave.

'Right guys,' said Mr Moore. 'We won't keep you guessing any longer. Here's what we're thinking.'

There were no real surprises, apart from some 'gender-blind casting', which meant that Tybalt was now a girl from Year Seven and Friar Lawrence had become a nun.

By the time he got to Mercutio (Pete Hughes – who else?) I was so excited, I wasn't thinking straight. With only a few parts left, I figured I was in with a chance.

'Okay people, it's time to meet our Romeo.' It wasn't exactly a TV talent show moment, but Mr Moore paused dramatically anyway. 'It's Duncan Fox.'

Romeo acknowledged his fans.

Mr Moore checked his watch. 'I'm afraid we've overrun a bit. Anyway, before I let you all go, I'm sure you want to find out who's playing Juliet. We talked a lot about this, didn't we, Fleur? But I think we got it right in the end.'

It might sound silly, but I really trusted Mr Moore to do the right thing.

This time he paused even longer. I sank my nails into the back of my wrist.

'Hannah, we'd like you to be our Juliet.'

And everyone cheered.

Duncan Fox was first to offer his congratulations, followed by practically half the cast wanting to hug Hannah to death. Only Miss Hoolyhan looked less than delighted. She pulled at her grand-piano earring, whispering agitatedly to Mr Moore.

'Hang on a minute,' he said. 'I'm afraid we've forgotten someone.' I was so gutted, I barely realised he was talking about me. 'We really liked your reading, Beth, so I'm sure you'll be pleased to hear that we've cast you as Juliet's Nurse.'

And if you must know, I wasn't exactly delirious about it. Hannah and Duncan might have had all the chemistry, but I'd set my mind on Juliet, and I was the best, I knew I was. And so did Mr Moore. In fact, I was so incensed I had this crazy urge to have it out with him in front of the whole cast. Fortunately, the mass exodus had started already. Mr Moore shouted after them as they stampeded into the corridor, 'Okay guys, if you haven't read the play yet, make sure you do. I'll have a rehearsal schedule up by tomorrow lunchtime.'

At first I felt like crying. The Nurse was an old woman; worse than that, a *comedy* old woman. It was pretty insulting when you thought about it.

It was only as I trudged past the car park that I started to see things differently. Juliet and the Nurse had at least three good scenes together. Three perfect bonding opportunities for me, Hannah and Mr Moore.

And another thing: who was the first person Juliet

turned to in a crisis? It wasn't Romeo, and it certainly wasn't her parents. No, it was the person who'd looked after her since she was a baby, the one person she really trusted – her beloved Nurse. Okay, it was a bit of a long shot, but maybe, just maybe, some of that closeness could spill over into real life.

Most of the others were climbing into warm cars. Hannah was shivering at the bus stop, texting furiously. She looked pretty fed up for someone who'd just got the lead part in a world famous tragedy. Even so, I couldn't pass up the opportunity to talk to her.

'Well done for getting Juliet.'

'Thanks,' she said, stabbing her phone like she wanted to kill it. 'I don't know why he picked me anyway. You were way better than I was.'

'No . . . *no*,' I lied. 'You were . . . perfect. Anyway, I'm going to be the Nurse, so we'll have lots to do together.'

Hannah didn't look that thrilled. 'I haven't even read it yet. I was going to last night, but I had to babysit my stupid stepbrother again.'

'I'm really looking forward to it, aren't you?'

'Yeah . . . kind of,' said Hannah, as a clapped-out Astra with a dented bumper pulled up alongside us and the tinted front window slid down.

Mr Moore was in the driver's seat. 'Night girls, hope you enjoyed yourselves back there.'

'Yeah, brilliant,' I said, trying to identify the ancient song on his car stereo.

Mr Moore coughed nervously. 'I don't know what you

said to him, Hannah, but thanks for talking to Mr . . . Whathisname.'

'No problem. Catchpole's a right dick.'

Mr Moore tried hard not to smile.

I'd been wanting to tell him all week. 'I saw your poem on YouTube, sir.' (Thanks to Grunt, the whole school had; and the female half was pretty impressed.) 'I thought it was . . . excellent . . . really powerful.'

'At least someone does,' said Mr Moore. 'Anyway, I'd better get going. See you both later.'

His car spluttered forward, picking up speed as it pulled out of the main gate.

'Nice, isn't he?'

'Okay, I suppose,' said Hannah, still glaring into her mobile. 'Bit of a geek if you ask me.'

Conversations
We Never Had

Just lately, I'd had this real urge to talk about Mum. Dad tried to pretend he never thought about her, but every once in a while his eyes would come to rest on one of her books (*Le Rouge et Le Noir*, *50 Children's Party Cakes*) and suddenly you'd see this shiver of recognition.

Sometimes I'd try to ambush him, slipping it randomly into the conversation so it was harder to change the subject. He always managed though. And it was the same old story the night he arrived back from LA and presented me with an expensive-looking carrier bag.

'Thanks Dad,' I said, taking out a pair of purple baggy trousers. 'What are they?'

'You mean, you don't know?'

'Not really.'

'Biker sweat pants from Aviator Nation,' he said proudly. 'Nikki in cabin crew told me you'd love them.'

If I was a registered clown perhaps. 'Thanks Dad, they're really . . .' I slung them over the back of the sofa, a little depressed by the $199.99 price tag.

'So, how have you been?' he said. 'Parties every night, I suppose?'

'Nice one, Dad.'

We sat at opposite ends of the sofa, like strangers at the dentist.

'What *have* you been up to then?'

I was dying to tell him. So how come a little voice was urging me not to? 'Well there is one thing. I'm going to be in the school play.'

Yes that was it – his look of sheer astonishment when I said it. 'Really, what part?'

'It's Shakespeare, *Romeo and Juliet*. I'm going to be playing the Nurse.'

'And you're all right with that, are you?'

'Yeah, why shouldn't I be?'

'I still haven't forgotten that poor innkeeper,' said Dad with a sickly smile. 'No wonder he only let you sleep in the stable.'

'I'll be fine. I'm actually really looking forward to it.'

Dad seemed genuinely pleased for me. 'You'll be following in the family tradition then. I used to do a bit of acting myself.'

It was another chance to ambush him. 'So did Mum, didn't she? Weren't you in a play together at college?'

His mouth fell open; eventually half a sentence popped out. '*Waiting for Godot*, it was quite . . .'

'I'd love to hear about it, Dad. Have you got any photos?'

He jumped off the sofa like a certified dentophobic, grabbed his suitcase and yawned theatrically. 'I'm sorry Beth, I'm too tired right now. I'll see you in the morning.'

'Oh come on, Dad. I only want to talk about her.'

'I'm not sure I can —'

'You haven't forgotten about the eighteenth, have you? You do remember what day it is?'

'Of course I haven't forgotten,' he whispered. 'Now if you don't mind, I'm going to bed.'

'Please Dad. I just need to —'

'And don't forget to buy me a ticket for the play.' He stood in the doorway, perfectly poised for a quick getaway. 'I've always been partial to a good tragedy.'

My dad was not an easy man to talk to, unlike Mr Moore.

Why Do Fools
Fall In Love?

We spent most of the first rehearsal talking about the play. Mr Moore insisted that the whole production team should be there. From Romeo and Juliet to Mrs Gough, her scenery painters and the girls designing the website, we were 'all in it together', so it was important that everyone could have their say.

And it sounded like a good idea until the assistant lighting designer slumped into the empty chair next to me. 'Who does he think he is anyway,' whispered Grunt, 'Martin Scorsese?'

'Shhh, I'm trying to listen.'

'We want to set the play in 1960s Brighton,' said Mr Moore. 'Now, has anyone heard of the mods and rockers?'

Not a hand reached for the sky.

'Well, they were basically two conflicting strands of British youth sub-culture.' Some of the Year Eights looked bored already. 'The mods were clean-cut types who often rode motor scooters and were into soul music and ska. The rockers preferred black leather jackets and motorcycle boots – and of course, they were crazy about rock and roll.'

'Sweet,' said Pete Hughes. 'What about their hair?'

'Greased back with a teddy-boy quiff,' said Mrs Gough, who looked old enough to remember.

Mr Moore nodded excitedly. 'The point is they *hated* each other – just like the two families in the play. In fact, sometimes they'd ride down to Brighton for these massive gang fights.' Some of the boys perked up a bit. 'That's why we're going to make the Monatagues rockers and the Capulets mods.'

'If it's all set in the sixties, how are we going to do the sword fights?' said Duncan Fox.

Mr Moore's innovative – others might say suicidal – choice of fight arranger had obviously been doing his homework for once. 'Bike chains and flick knives,' said Dave Denyer. 'Maybe even a couple of deckchairs.'

Miss Hoolyhan sounded unconvinced. 'We'll have to see about that, David. Of course there's a lot we can do with the music. Ska is a very —'

'Okay, guys,' said Mr Moore, jumping in quickly. 'Who wants to share their first responses to the play? Yes, Beth.'

I really wanted to please him, so it was lucky I'd read

the introduction as many times as the play. 'The poetry's amazing. I love the way he switches between comedy and tragedy to heighten the tension. And his use of some of the minor characters is masterly.'

'Masterly,' echoed that boy from the wind band who got his picture in *The County Times* when his bees escaped.

'Thank you, Beth,' said Mr Moore. 'That was very . . . How about someone else?'

'Don't you think it's a bit unrealistic?' said the girl playing Lady Montague. 'Juliet's got all these blokes after her, and the dumb mare goes for the one person she can't have.'

I liked the way Mr Moore laughed. It was boyish, but not juvenile; infectious, but never cruel. 'I think that's the point, Magda. Shakespeare's saying you can't help who you fall in love with.'

Miss Hoolyhan was with him all the way. 'Oh yes, absolutely.'

Magda looked less certain. 'Even if they did feel that way about each other, I just don't think they'd be stupid enough to kill themselves.'

'It's not stupid,' said a voice. 'If you really loved someone, you couldn't live without them.' Hannah sounded almost like she was talking from experience. As usual, she was about half a centimetre from Duncan Fox. Putting two and two together was depressingly easy.

In fact, it was so depressing I barely noticed the

strange spectacle of Grunt with his hand in the air. 'It's a bit disgusting, isn't it, sir?

'How do you mean, George?'

'Juliet's only thirteen, but her mum and dad want to marry her off to some old count. That's well out of order.'

There followed ten minutes of fruitless discussion in which the subjects of celebrity power couples, the latest suspected Year Nine pregnancy and the final episode of *The Sopranos* were all deemed somehow relevant.

'Thank you everyone; that was fascinating,' said Mr Moore.

'If you say so,' muttered the *County Times* bee boy.

'Now, for the last twenty minutes, Miss Hoolyhan's going to take the Chorus to a practice room to get started on the music while I do some character work here. Which means the rest of you technical guys can head off.'

'I'll wait for you if you like,' said Grunt.

'*No*,' I said, grabbing the one foolproof excuse I could think of. 'I'm going to pop into town for some shopping. I need a new bra.'

Grunt grabbed his Grateful Dead duffel bag. 'Fair enough, I'll see you tomorrow then.' He was still making sarcastic comments about my 'new friend' Hannah. If he found out I was planning to ambush her at the bus stop again, he'd have a field day.

'There are two ways of building a character,' said Mr Moore. 'You can either start from the inside, or concentrate on externals – like a regional accent for instance, or the way you walk.'

Mr Moore seemed to favour a mixture of both. First we worked on how our characters would perform everyday tasks. I couldn't really see the point of knowing how the Nurse cleaned her teeth or peeled a banana, but it was far less painful than what happened next.

'This exercise is dead simple,' said Mr Moore. 'What I want you to do is jot down all the reasons you think you might be suitable for the part we've given you. It's about finding stuff inside yourself that's going to help you understand your character.'

Duncan Fox was scribbling on the back of his Science book. '*Good kisser?*' giggled Hannah. 'You can't put that.'

Mr Moore was not amused. 'Come on guys, this is serious. Find yourselves a quiet spot on the floor and really give it some thought.'

I'd bought myself a fake leather notebook to use as a rehearsal diary. It was the first time I'd opened it, and I was already suffering from writer's block.

Mr Moore walked among us, checking out what we'd written. 'That's interesting, Clinton. I suppose an apothecary might very well keep bees.'

An unaccompanied – and appropriately tragic – version of 'Only Fools Fall in Love' floated across from the practice studios.

'Relax,' said Mr Moore. 'Don't force it. Just let your minds go blank and see where it leads you.'

I should never have done what he asked. Letting my

guard down was a big mistake. Even the job title made me shudder.

'And don't worry what you come up with at this stage. You may not know what you're looking for.'

Mr Moore was standing over me. I sensed his presence like a shaft of sunlight on my back.

'Not written anything yet, Beth? It's okay – it's fine. Just free associate for a minute. What's the first thing you think of when you hear the word "nurse"?'

For some people it probably sounded warm and comforting; for me it meant a fluorescently lit corridor and people whispering behind my back. I knew they were different kinds of nurses, but I couldn't help thinking of Mum. A surgeon's knife twisted in my stomach; seconds later a barrage of tears was exploding on the empty white pages of my rehearsal diary.

'Are you okay?' Mr Moore sounded miles away. 'Look, it's really no biggie. It doesn't matter if you can't think of anything.'

That wasn't the problem. I couldn't *stop* thinking. Once I was in that corridor I had to keep walking. Sooner or later I'd reach the door at the end. 'I'm okay,' I sobbed, half aware of how silly it sounded. 'I'm just a bit . . .'

'Take a deep breath,' whispered Mr Moore, his hand resting lightly on my shoulder. 'You'll be fine in a minute.' He turned to the others. 'Okay guys, I think we'll leave it there. Beth's feeling a bit woozy.'

They crowded around me, offering amateur diagnoses

and character assassinations: 'Call old Catchpole, she's probably on drugs.' 'Call the vet; she's got that mad cow thing.' 'Call the midwife you mean.' 'Talk about drama queen.'

At least *one* of them sounded sympathetic. 'Shut up you lot,' said Hannah. 'Can't you see she's upset?'

'Give her some space,' said Mr Moore. 'Now, *please*, you're really not helping here. Just grab your bags and be as quiet as you can on the way out. Tomorrow lunchtime we'll start work on the opening fight sequence.'

And at last they were gone, their belligerent chatter fading to a distant moan.

I felt much better now it was just Mr Moore and me. 'I ought to be going too,' I said, trying to climb to my feet, but feeling all wobbly.

'Don't stand up too quickly. You'll get dizzy.'

'It's okay, sir, I'm fine.'

'You don't look fine,' he said, offering me his hand. 'I think you'd better come and sit in my office for five minutes. You look like you could use a cup of tea.'

The office had certainly changed since Miss Carver's day. Apart from the lumpy armchair, which was still as uncomfortable as it looked, the pungent aroma of her perfume had been supplanted by a delicious combination of freshly ground coffee and aftershave, and the walls hidden by a gallery of theatre bills and a huge poster of an ancient looking band called The Cure.

'I'm probably their biggest fan,' said Mr Moore, drowning a tea bag in boiling water and squeezing it against the side of the mug with a teaspoon. 'You must have heard "Boys Don't Cry".'

I wished I could have said yes. 'I don't think so.'

'You should have a listen. I've seen them live, like, thirty times.' He handed me a mug with the singer's face on it.

'Thanks, I will.'

Mr Moore sat on the front of his desk, gently swinging one leg. 'Are you feeling better now?'

I nodded.

'Acting exercises sometimes unleash very powerful emotions. Don't worry, it happens all the time.'

If he carried on being so nice to me, I'd probably start crying again. 'Thanks.'

'Do you want to talk about it?'

If I could have talked to anyone it would probably have been Mr Moore. 'I can't.'

'That's fine,' he said. 'But my office is always open if you change your mind.'

'Why Do Fools Fall in Love' didn't seem to be getting much better. Miss Hoolyhan was thumping out the tune on the piano.

'Thanks, Mr Moore.'

'Look, I don't know what it's all about, Beth, but if you'd rather not carry on with the play, I'd quite understand.'

'No, no . . . *no*, I mean . . . no, I'll be fine, I was just feeling a bit . . .'

Mr Moore launched himself off the front of his desk,

pulling up about two centimetres in front of me. 'That's great. I'd hate to lose you, of course.'

The music died suddenly. My eyes were drawn to the poster on the wall behind him:

POETRY NIGHT:
SIX GREAT POETS
AND A LOT OF WORDS

'That's not you is it, sir? I know you write poetry.'

He nodded shyly. 'It's a gig I'm doing in Brighton. Just some local writers in a room over a pub.'

'Sounds brilliant. I'd really like to come down and support you.'

'I don't know about that, Beth. I mean, you'd have to ask your parents first. And I'd rather you didn't mention it to the others. It's still work in progress you see.'

It was three weekends away. I did a quick mental calculation. Dad wouldn't be flying again until the Tuesday. He'd never let me go on my own. 'Well, good luck with it anyway.'

And I was just about to tell him how talented I thought he was, when the door flew open and in burst Miss Hoolyhan. 'Are you all right?'

'Beth had a little moment in the rehearsal,' said Mr Moore. 'But she's fine now.'

Miss Hoolyhan sounded relieved. 'Yes, Hannah told me what happened. She was obviously worried about you.'

'How did the singing go?' said Mr Moore. 'It sounded great from here.'

'It was fine,' snapped Miss Hoolyhan. 'Anyway Beth, you'd better be getting home. Your dad will be wondering where you've got to.'

'Yes, miss. And thanks, sir. I feel a lot better now.'

'Take care, Beth,' said Mr Moore. 'And try not to worry, yeah?'

By the time I got to the courtyard, there were the early warning signs of a smile on my face. Hannah would be on her bus by now. That was a shame. But it didn't stop me feeling more positive about the whole friendship thing. After all, who'd been so worried about me that she'd run all the way to the practice rooms to tell Miss Hoolyhan? It was Hannah. Whichever way you looked at it, it had to be a good sign.

But there was more to the upturned corners of my mouth than that. He wasn't like the others. They talked at you for five minutes and sent you away with a cliché in your ear: *Time is a great healer. What doesn't kill you only makes you stronger. It's okay to feel angry.* Mr Moore was different. He actually listened. And unlike the head of Year Eleven and the acting director of Student Welfare, his office was always open.

There was something else, too. And it was getting harder to ignore. Every time Mr Moore came near me, a swarm of butterflies took flight in my chest and I wanted to . . . I was going to say 'laugh', but if such a thing was actually possible, it would have been more like laughing and crying at the same time.

And I'd be lying if I said I didn't have a pretty good idea what it meant. The answer to my question was getting clearer by the minute: whichever way you looked at it, it was almost certainly wrong to feel that way about a teacher.

The Best
Metaphors

Three weeks later, I still hadn't talked to Mr Moore –
not properly anyway. I'd stood outside his office several
times, but I'd never found the courage to knock. As for
Hannah, it was great rehearsing together, but she spent
most of the time glued to Duncan Fox or 'working on
her character'. She was brilliant by the way. When she
acted, you forgot she was this amazingly sophisticated
Year Eleven. All you saw was a naive thirteen-year-old
who'd fallen in love for the first time.

But my life hadn't changed a bit. Dad was as
uncommunicative as ever, and I was still walking home
with Grunt. He'd taken to staying behind after school
to 'computerise the lighting system'. At the end of every
rehearsal he'd be waiting for me, like one of those scruffy
dogs you see tied up outside OneStop.

So how did we end up on the 6.55 train to Brighton one Saturday night? Simple really: Dad would never have let me go alone. He was quite happy to fly halfway round the world every month, but the rest of the time he tried to play the possessive father. That's why I'd asked Grunt. He was the sort of teenage boy that dads instinctively trusted their teenage daughters with.

And talk about strangers on a train. For reasons best known to himself, Grunt had abandoned his baggy vagrant look in favour of skinny black chinos, a smart corduroy jacket and a suspiciously well-ironed black shirt. We'd known each other since the dawn of the century, but the conversation was more stilted than a colony of jugglers.

'Hey, Beth, I just wanted to say that . . .'

'Yes.'

'You look really . . .'

'What?' I said frostily.

He sank back onto his bum-numbingly uncomfortable seat. 'Nothing.'

I stared out at the flashing countryside, daydreaming about Mr Moore; a strange combination of excitement and fear.

'Hey Beth.'

'What is it now?'

He had a weird smile on his face. I didn't like the look of it at all. 'What do you call a mushroom that drives a Ferrari?'

If I kept quiet maybe he wouldn't tell me.

Halfway to the ticket barrier, Grunt's warped sense of humour went into overdrive. It was such a shock that I had to double check he was actually holding my hand.

'What are you playing at? Trying to be funny are you?'

'Yeah . . . that's right,' said Grunt, loosening his sweaty grip with an unconvincing chuckle. 'Sorry, just . . . messing with you.'

'Well it's not funny.'

'No.'

We turned out of the station into a murky tunnel. A man in a sleeping bag was serenading his drowsy dog on the harmonica. Two minutes later we were surrounded by trendy gift shops.

'That's it,' said Grunt, pointing at the pub on the corner. 'The Cape of Good Hope.'

A familiar figure was hovering outside. 'What's *she* doing here?' said Grunt.

Miss Hoolyhan was wearing a long flowery skirt. Festooned with bracelets and her dyed black hair swept back at an improbable angle, she looked like a white witch in a wind tunnel. 'Hello, you two. You're here to support Mr Moore, I suppose.' She tugged at her purple silk scarf. 'Parking in this place is a nightmare. I'm right down on the seafront.'

The poetry gig was in a room above the bar. A bearded man with a cash box was waiting at the top of the stairs.

'You students?' he said. '*No*, not you love.'

Miss Hoolyhan's smile wilted. 'We're here to support a colleague of mine.'

'Right – well it's a tenner for adults and five quid concessions.'

Miss Hoolyhan reached into her wicker handbag. I paid for Grunt and me. It was part of the deal.

'Very twenty-first century,' said the man on the door. 'You want to hang on to her, matey. She's a keeper.'

'Yes,' said Grunt, gloomily.

The room smelled of fried food. There was a tiny stage down one end with a microphone at the front.

Grunt's mood improved slightly. 'Don't think much of the lighting.'

Judging by the rest of the audience – a select group of vintage eccentrics in eccentric vintage clothing – Miss Hoolyhan would blend in nicely. It was the young girl at the table by the window, sipping mineral water and looking typically gorgeous in her greeny-blue top that looked out of place.

'Hi Hannah,' I said, waving at her through the gloom, delighted she was on her own for once. 'Good to see you.'

She didn't wave back. 'Yeah . . . hi.'

Miss Hoolyhan made a beeline for her table. 'How are rehearsals going? Mr Moore says you're a wonderful Juliet.'

'Really?' said Hannah.

'Three cheers for Martin bloody Scorsese,' muttered Grunt.

I flashed him my dirtiest frown. 'Okay if we join you, Hannah?'

'Yeah . . . fine.'

'Didn't realise you were coming,' I said.

'Duncan wanted to,' said Hannah. 'Nothing to do with me.'

I thought it was too good to be true. Duncan Fox had emerged from a door marked *Private* with a pint glass in his hand. He acknowledged our arrival with a princely yawn and squeezed in beside Hannah. 'What's this then, the Steve Moore Appreciation Society?'

Miss Hoolyhan reached for her charm bracelet. 'Well *I'm* here for the poetry.' I don't think she even convinced herself. 'Anyway Duncan, are you sure you should be drinking that?'

'It's Diet Coke, miss. Mr Moore got it for me.'

Miss Hoolyhan's face flared delightedly. 'Where is he?'

'He's through that door, getting ready,' said Duncan.

'Perhaps I should go and wish him luck,' said Miss Hoolyhan. 'He told me how nervous he gets.'

'*No*,' said Hannah. 'He said he wanted to do a warm-up.'

Grunt rolled his eyes at me. 'It'll take more than a warm-up.'

'Oh shut up,' I said. 'The show's about to start.'

Mr Moore wasn't on until the second half, which was fine because I was so excited about seeing him that I needed to calm down. And some of the others were actually quite good: 'Murdo the Actuary' recited 'Twenty-four Limericks About Assisted Suicide', a transsexual by the name of the Reverend Harry Fowler covered her mouth in Sellotape and encouraged the whole audience to join her in 'Two Minutes' Silence', and Sally Webb read a haiku about her menstrual cycle entitled 'Girl on a Red Bike'.

I could almost hear the running commentary in Grunt's head, and 'Romeo and Juliet' were so busy whispering that I doubt they even heard most of it. At the interval, I tried talking to Hannah about our scenes in the play, but she soon disappeared to the Ladies, leaving Duncan Fox playing killing games on his phone.

I'd always liked Miss Hoolyhan. She was the only one who didn't try to smother me when my mum died. After the second poem about childbirth, she slipped down to the bar and bought us all drinks. But there was something deeply unhealthy about the way she idolised Mr Moore. It was sad to watch a woman of her age making such a fool of herself. You should have seen her face when he finally jumped onto the stage.

'Hi guys. The name's Moore, Steve Moore, and I'm a poet. This first one's called "Grown-up".'

I was probably biased, but it seemed to me that Mr Moore was on a completely different level. He took ordinary things like takeaway food and junk mail and made you see them in a whole new way. But it was his last poem that really spoke to me.

'This is a new one,' he said, looking nervous for the

71

first time. 'It's called "The Best Metaphors Are Taken".'

Duncan and Hannah were drowning in mutual admiration; Grunt attempted to flick beer mats into his empty glass; Miss Hoolyhan and I sat transfixed.

'My love is the dead pigeon in the wheelie bin,
(You swept me away)
My love is terminal cancer,
(Nothing could make it better)
My love is a steaming pile of dog's vomit,
(I will always return to it)
My love is the hangman's noose,
(When I fall you hold me tighter)

But I can never tell you, no, I can never tell you,
Because the best metaphors are taken.'

At first I'd thought it was just a feature of his writing; the way it felt like he was speaking directly to you. But maybe it was more than that; maybe this time he actually *was*. A warm tingly sensation was flooding over me, and with it the birth of an intoxicating idea. What if he'd guessed how I felt about him? What if the 'love poem' was Mr Moore's way of showing me that he felt the same? Well he was a teacher; he couldn't make an announcement in the middle of a lesson.

And just before he left the stage with a shy, 'I've been Steve Moore, you've been fantastic, thank you and goodnight,' he as good as confirmed it by glancing across at me and making my evening with an enormous smile.

I almost felt sorry for Miss Hoolyhan. The poor deluded woman obviously thought it was directed at her. After the show, when he came out to meet us clutching a bottle of mineral water, she was all over him like childhood eczema.

'That was wonderful Steve,' she drooled. 'The love poem was so clever.'

'It was amazing,' I said, trying to show him that I understood. 'Thanks . . . sir. You really are incredibly talented.'

Mr Moore turned to Duncan and Hannah. 'How about you guys?'

Duncan Fox suppressed a giggle. 'Well, it was certainly . . . different.'

'Hannah?' said Mr Moore.

'Yeah . . . it was all right.' She shrugged. 'I liked the one about the accountant in space.'

He didn't ask Grunt.

'You staying for a drink, Steve?' said Miss Hoolyhan. 'I'd love to talk some more about it.'

Mr Moore took a swig of mineral water. 'Sorry, Fleur, but I really should get going. The parking in this town's insane.'

'Yes, yes of course,' said Miss Hoolyhan. 'Goodnight then. And thanks for a . . . goodnight.'

Mr Moore looked relieved as the top of her hair disappeared down the stairs. 'Now what about you guys? You came on the train, didn't you? I said I'd take these

73

two. Would you like a lift?'

'No thanks,' said Grunt. 'I think we'd rather —'

There was no way he was getting away with that. 'Thank you, Mr Moore, we'd love one.'

And there it was again; the same tingly feeling when he caught my eye. I knew it was wrong. But it just felt so, well, right. My heart was doing gymnastics all the way to the car park. Like the poem said, he could never '*tell*' me, but sooner or later he'd make it obvious how he felt. It was just a case of finding the right moment. Why else was he so keen to offer me a lift? Why else would he have written 'The Best Metaphors Are Taken'?

The horrible truth was lurking behind the tinted rear windows of his car.

'I'll have to put the baby seat in the boot,' he said. 'Then three of you can squeeze in the back.'

It hadn't even crossed my mind that Mr Moore might be married. In the backstory I'd created for him, he was a lonely bachelor in a tiny flat full of classic paperbacks. I should have known that someone like him would never be alone. Even so, I had to be sure. 'Couldn't your wife make it then, sir?'

'Sarah and I aren't actually married,' he said, dumping the baby seat in the boot.

'But you've got a kid,' said Grunt, helpfully. 'So you might as well be.'

'Yes,' said Mr Moore. 'And you're right, Beth. Archie's teething so Sarah didn't want to leave him with a babysitter.'

My whole body seemed to freeze. There was no need for half a page of footnotes; it was just so humiliatingly obvious. The poem wasn't for me at all, it was for this Sarah person and the unfortunately-named Archie. There was no reason he should have told anyone, but I couldn't quite forgive him for keeping it so quiet.

'In you get then,' said Mr Moore, holding the seat back for Hannah. I tried to push in next to her, but Duncan Fox beat me to it.

Grunt looked very pleased with himself in the front seat. 'Nice car,' he said, smirking at me in the rear-view mirror to make sure I knew he was being 'funny'.

Mr Moore rummaged through his CD collection and put on some music.

I'd spent the afternoon researching them on YouTube. I recognised the jangly guitar sound and angsty synth. 'That's The Cure, isn't it, sir?'

'That's right,' he said, *do do*ing along with the singer. 'And by the way guys, call me Steve when we're out of school, yeah?' He turned up the volume. 'What do you think of them anyway?'

'They're great,' I lied, trying to hide the tears in my eyes.

'Surprisingly catchy for a depressing Goth pop outfit,' said Grunt.

'Yes,' said Mr Moore. 'They were practically the soundtrack to my adolescence. It kind of makes me feel like I'm young again.'

If it was the soundtrack to his adolescence he must

have had a pretty crap time. Perhaps we were all thinking the same thing because no one said a word for the next twenty minutes.

'So where do you guys live?' said Mr Moore after a while.

'Up by the station,' said Grunt. 'I'm a bit further down, but you can drop us off together if you like.'

'Cool,' said Mr Moore. 'You all right back there? Shall I turn the heater on?'

'Thanks, Steve,' said Hannah.

By the time he dropped us off, I was so depressed I just wanted to curl up and cry.

'Goodnight guys,' said Mr Moore. 'And thanks for coming tonight.'

Duncan and Hannah didn't even look up as the horrible little car spluttered away from the kerb.

And I was fumbling for my front door key when Grunt turned nasty.

Either his chinos were a size too small or he was bursting out of them like the Incredible Hulk. 'Well thanks for a great night.'

'What are you talking about?'

'You know what I'm talking about.'

'No I don't.'

Grunt snorted derisively. 'If it's not your "new friend Hannah" – who, by the way, is *so* not your friend – it's that Moore idiot.'

'What?'

It was a terrible impersonation: high-pitched and whiny, like a five-year-old. 'Oh Mr Moore, you're *so* lovely. I think you're the most talented man in the whole wide world.'

'Stop it.'

'I've seen the way you look at him.'

'I don't know what you're talking about.'

'Come off it, Beth. Even Stevie Wonder could see you've got a super-sized schoolgirl crush on him.'

Was it that obvious? 'Don't talk rubbish. He's a good teacher, that's all.'

'Are you sure about that?'

'Course.'

I'd never seen him look so serious. 'You should keep away from him, Beth. You'll only get hurt.'

It was probably the best advice he'd ever given me. Pity I took no notice.

Reality
Check

As soon as I walked into the canteen on Monday, I knew for certain that Grunt was right. Hannah was *so* never going to be my friend. I stood and watched her for a while, laughing and joking with Duncan and the rest of them, surreptitiously texting at the same time. That was her all over. She could barely keep up with the friends she had. No wonder she'd got no time for a new one.

And the happier she looked, the sadder it made me. My lame attempts to change my life had failed epically. Maybe it was time to accept defeat and not move on.

Grunt was waiting at our usual table, the hint of 'I told you so' playing about his tomato-purée stained lips. But I didn't want to give him the satisfaction, so I abandoned the dinner queue and headed out to the courtyard.

Miss Hoolyhan was staring at the recycling bins. She'd tamed her hair with an Alice band and her face was whiter than un-ruled A4. Avoiding her sad gaze, I gulped down a mouthful of air and turned towards the drama studio.

I still couldn't believe how stupid I'd been. Half the girls at St Thomas's had crushes on him, but I doubt even the most immature Year Seven had seriously thought that Mr Moore might like her back. It wasn't as if he'd led me on or anything. All he'd ever done was be kind to me. It was hardly his fault that I'd totally misread the signals.

And now I just wanted things to go back to the way they were. If I could just have a 'normal' conversation with him, maybe I could start getting over it.

His office door was open; it always was. Only a hand's width, but enough to spy on him all those times I'd been too scared to knock. He was communing with his laptop; tapping tensely, his face creased in concentration.

I knocked and went in.

'Beth, hi . . . didn't see you there. What can I . . .?'

'I just popped up to say thanks for the lift the other night. It was nice of you to go out of your way like that.'

'Oh right . . . no problem.'

He looked so tired. I suppose a new baby would do that to you. 'Are you all right . . . Steve?'

'I'm fine,' he said, closing his laptop and half smiling at me. 'I've got a lot on my mind right now.'

I wanted to touch him – just a reassuring hand on

the shoulder. But even that would have been what Mr Catchpole called 'inappropriate'. 'Is it about the play?'

'Yes . . . yes,' he said, rearranging his red and orange Post-it notes. 'There's such a lot to get through.'

'I think it's going really well. The fight scenes are amazing.'

'You're doing a great job yourself, Beth,' said Mr Moore. 'You have a very interesting quality on stage. It always feels like you're thinking so much more than you actually say.'

'Thank you.'

He reached for his ballpoint and started clicking. 'And how about you, Beth? You look kind of . . . restless. Is something bothering you?'

'I can see that you're busy. I'll come back another . . .'

'Go on,' he said. 'Take a seat. Tell me all about it.'

The lead singer of The Cure (Robert something or other) surveyed the scene through his smudged mascara and haystack hair. He was probably dreaming up a miserable song about us.

I parked myself on the ailing armchair. Mr Moore would have made a great interrogator. Suddenly I wanted to talk. 'It's nothing really. This time of year's always a bit hard for me.'

'Is this something to do with your mum, Beth?'

'How did you know about that?'

'Fleur Hoolyhan told me. She thought it might explain what happened at the rehearsal.'

I didn't know whether to be pleased that he knew,

or angry with Miss Hoolyhan for telling him. 'After it happened, I kind of cut myself off from everyone – didn't talk about it for ages. Just lately though, I really thought I was ready to makes some changes.'

'Yes,' said Mr Moore, thoughtfully. 'And sometimes it's hard to move on.'

'Tell me about it. I suppose that's why I wanted to be friends with Hannah.'

Mr Moore lined up his pencil holder with his Sellotape dispenser. 'What, Juliet Hannah, you mean?'

'It's one of the main reasons I signed up for the play. It seemed like a good way of getting to know her. Believe it or not, I actually thought it might work.'

'I never liked school much myself,' said Mr Moore. 'If you weren't into sport, they all assumed you were a weirdo. All I really liked was acting.'

'Just like Hannah; she's brilliant, isn't she? Except it's not really acting, is it?'

'What do you mean?'

'Well she's in love, isn't she? It's so obvious.'

'Is it?' said Mr Moore, sweeping paperclips into his cupped hand.

'Well you've seen them together – Duncan and her.'

He stopped sweeping. 'Well, they're certainly very —'

'You must have noticed the way she flirts with him in rehearsals.'

'To be honest, Beth, I try to concentrate on the poetry.'

'No wonder she's got no time for anyone else.'

Mr Moore thought for a moment, pressing his index finger into the bridge of his nose. 'I suppose so. But I wouldn't give up completely. I don't see why you and Hannah *couldn't* be friends. You're both into acting, aren't you?'

'Thanks . . . Mr Moore. I know you're trying to be nice, but it's never going to happen, is it? It would take a complete miracle. And I really don't believe in them.'

ACT THREE

Miracle
at St Thomas's

Tuesday lunchtime, and I was freezing to death at the Millennium Pagoda, surrounded by the usual collection of social misfits.

I couldn't face the canteen. Grunt was lying in wait for me, and the thought of running into Hannah and her friends was even worse. So I squeezed into an empty picnic table, trying to pretend I was invisible. And what better way than to take out that stupid phone for practically the first time since my birthday, and stare into it like the rest of them.

'I've been looking everywhere for you.'

I knew the voice, but I couldn't place it. It didn't belong there. So I got the shock of my life when I saw who it was. 'Eh, what . . . *Why?* We haven't got a rehearsal, have we?'

'Relax,' smiled Hannah. 'I just want to ask you something.'

No wonder I was suspicious. It had all the makings of one of those 'get the geek' games that St Thomas's was famous for. 'What about?'

'Don't worry, it's nothing bad or anything. Now are you going to let me sit down or not?'

Why was she smiling so much? Another possibility sprang to mind. 'Have you been talking to Mr Moore?'

'Now why would I do that?'

'I don't know, it's just that . . . What do you want anyway?'

Hannah slipped into the seat opposite. 'I've got a favour to ask.'

'Yeah, sure, what is it?'

'You doing anything after school tonight?'

When was the secret cameraman going to jump out? 'Why?'

'Do you want to come round mine and rehearse a couple of scenes?'

I must have misheard. Had she just . . . 'Eh?'

'We've got the first run-through in a couple of weeks. I'm getting really nervous about it.'

I didn't know what to say.

'You'll probably need to ask someone first,' continued Hannah. 'We could do it another time if you like.'

'No, no, it's fine,' I said, jumping in before she could change her mind. 'My dad's in Bangkok anyway. I mean, I'd love to, Hannah. It sounds . . . perfect.'

And it was as easy as that. We arranged to meet under the conker tree just outside the main gate. And after she'd admired my phone for the second time, Hannah insisted on swapping numbers.

It was almost how I'd imagined it. Maybe that's why I didn't stop to consider how strange it was; how downright astonishing that Hannah Taylor should suddenly be so keen for my company. Or if I did, I smothered the idea at birth. Because nothing was going to stop me enjoying the moment; the moment when I knew for certain that Hannah and I would be friends.

Fool's Paradise

'Thought it was you. Why are you hanging about here?'

'I'm waiting for someone.'

'Hiding more likely,' said Grunt. 'Look, if you don't want to walk home with me, you only have to say.'

'It's not that, I —'

'Have I done something wrong?' His hand tightened around the cord of his Grateful Dead duffel bag. 'It wasn't the . . . what happened at Brighton Station, was it? You don't need to worry about that. Like I said, I was just having a laugh.'

I checked out the stragglers – the last dribs of St Thomas's Community College in their drab blue uniforms. Hannah was already fifteen minutes late. It was getting darker, just like my thoughts: *Why hasn't she texted me? What if she doesn't turn up?* 'No, it's not that. I —'

'And all that stuff about Mr Moore. I didn't really mean it. He's an okay bloke – if you're into that kind of thing.'

'Look I told you. I really am waiting for someone.'

'Who, Godot?' said Grunt, who couldn't grovel for two minutes without turning into a smart arse. 'I've read that play, Beth – half of it anyway. And let me tell you something – he *doesn't* turn up.'

'What, so no one could possibly be interested in me? Is that what you're saying?'

A pulse of anxiety rippled his chubby features. 'It's not someone in the play, is it?'

'Could be.'

'Not that kid in the skiffle group?'

'Nope.'

'Or the guy playing Montague?'

'*No.*'

He could hardly bear to say it. 'Don't tell me it's Dave Denyer.'

Even I had to smile at that one. 'It's Hannah, okay? I'm waiting for Hannah.'

Grunt threw back his head, braying with laughter, like an over-excited Year Seven at the war graves trip talent night. 'Yeah right, nice one Beth. Look I told you, if you don't want to walk with me that's fine.'

'It's true,' I said, a lot less confident than twenty minutes earlier. 'We're going back to hers to rehearse.'

'Yeah, course you are.'

'What's that supposed to mean?'

Grunt could be every bit as sarcastic and patronising as some of the teachers. 'You don't think it's a bit odd then – that she didn't ask her beloved Duncan? Come on Beth, it's another one of their wind-ups.'

'Well maybe I got the wrong . . .'

And then I saw her, stumbling towards me across the damp grass in her non-regulation heels, her dazzling smile illuminating the early evening mist.

'Hope I'm not interrupting anything,' said Hannah, smiling.

Grunt looked like he'd seen a ghost.

'You're not,' I said, just a tiny bit triumphantly. 'George was leaving, weren't you?'

Grunt winced like a wounded bloodhound and turned away. I couldn't help feeling sorry for him. 'See you, Beth. Hope the rehearsal goes . . .' His voice vanished as I basked in Hannah's captivating presence.

'Sorry I'm late,' she said. 'Catchpole caught me texting in History so he confiscated my phone. I was supposed to see him in the staffroom after school, but he didn't turn up for hours. That's why I couldn't text you.'

'It's okay.' I smiled, half aware that Grunt was lolloping languidly down the hill. 'I'm just glad you're here now.'

Walking home with Hannah felt like the most natural thing in the world.

'It must be so great, having a dad who's a pilot,' she said. 'Do you get cheap flights?'

It wasn't something I liked admitting, but I already figured I could trust Hannah. 'Well, I would do only . . . you won't believe this, but I'm actually a bit scared of flying. He took me to Paris last summer. But we had to go on Eurostar.'

To Grunt it was one of life's most pleasing ironies; Hannah barely cracked a smile. 'That's a shame. Flying's amazing.'

She was so easy to talk to. By the time we reached her house, in one of those new cul-de-sacs near the Sports Centre, we'd covered everything from Mr Catchpole's sense-of-humour bypass to that new telly programme where celebrities teach teenage mothers their favourite pasta recipes.

Hannah's mum was making biscuits. She worked as a teaching assistant at that primary school where the deputy head got arrested. I was so keen to make a good impression that my lips were locked in a wide-mouthed smile. But I needn't have worried.

'This is my friend, Beth,' said Hannah, almost like I'd written the script myself.

'Hi Beth,' said her mum, waving at me with a tartan oven glove. 'I'm Steph by the way. Nice to meet you.' It was obvious where Hannah got her good looks. She was the sort of mum you saw in adverts for cleaning products.

'Hello Mrs Taylor,' I said, sounding more like an over-polite eight-year-old at a kids' party.

'Actually it's Mrs Poole,' she said. 'Beth's dad and I

aren't together any more.'

'Leave it out, Mum,' said Hannah. 'Beth doesn't want to hear about your sordid love life.'

Steph Poole smiled indulgently. 'Anyway, how was school? Hannah never tells me anything.'

'For goodness' sake, Mum. Shut up, why don't you?'

'School was fine,' I said, surprised to detect a note of sadness in my voice. The smell of freshly baked biscuits had triggered a half-forgotten memory. If I stopped to savour it, there was every chance I'd make a fool of myself. 'And the play's going really well. At least, it seems to be.'

'Well it ought to be with all the rehearsals you've been having.'

Two nights a week and a couple of lunchtimes didn't seem that excessive for a five-act tragedy, but she was probably one of those parents with a homework fetish.

'Hannah's going to be *so* brilliant as Juliet.'

'When is this play anyway? Hannah still hasn't told us.'

'It's the second to last week of term,' I said. 'The twenty-fourth to the twenty-sixth.'

'I'll write that down,' said Hannah's mum, turning to March in The Simpsons' Family Organiser on the fridge door and scrawling three black Xs in Lisa Simpson's column. 'Alan will have to check if he's working.'

'I told you, Mum,' said Hannah, 'don't bother.'

'Which reminds me, Al's going to be late tonight so we won't be eating until about half seven.'

'Typical,' said Hannah. 'I'm starving.'

'Take some biscuits if you're hungry.'

Hannah dumped her school bag in the middle of the kitchen floor and swept an armful of Viennese Fingers into a plastic container. 'Come on, Beth, let's go upstairs.'

'Thanks, er, Steph, I —'

Hannah grabbed my arm and led me out through the lounge. A boy in a primary school sweatshirt was waving a controller at an over-sized telly.

'That's my stepbrother,' she said. 'Nathan likes to spend his time slaughtering giant eyeballs.'

'Shut up,' said the kid with the controller. 'I'm in combat mode.'

'Pain-in-the-butt mode more likely,' said Hannah.

'Give us a biscuit,' said her stepbrother.

'Get one yourself,' said Hannah, giving him the (Viennese) finger.

'Your bum'll only get even bigger if you eat them all.'

'Yeah, and you'll only get dumber,' said Hannah, turning to me with a deafening stage whisper. 'Poor kid can hardly read.'

'At least I don't smell of dog poo.'

It sounded like a routine they'd been rehearsing for months. I was glad to escape upstairs.

Hannah's bedroom wasn't how I'd imagined it. There were a couple of mean-looking rappers on the wall and some digital grooming products whose uses I could only guess at, but for the most sophisticated girl in Year Eleven, the Disney memorabilia and bed strewn with

93

beanie babies came as quite a surprise.

Hannah was studying her bum in the dressing-table mirror. 'Sorry about that.'

'That's okay,' I said, wondering for the first time if she wasn't quite as confident as she seemed. 'I like your mum.'

'She's all right I suppose.'

'And what about Alan; is he your stepfather?'

Her face froze in the mirror. 'Yeah. Could we not talk about him, please?'

Perhaps I should have pressed her. I'd seen the way she tensed up when I mentioned him, but I didn't dare ruin the moment. 'What about your real dad, where's he?'

'Divorced and living in Milton Keynes,' said Hannah. 'That's what it says on his Facebook page.'

It sounded like the title of a bad novel. It was certainly enough to stifle the conversation. The cloud I was floating on seemed to have hit turbulence.

'Can I ask you something, Hannah?'

'Sure?'

'Why did you invite me here?'

'I told you. So we can work on our scenes together. This play's really important to me. I don't want to let anyone down.'

'I know,' I said, a faint shadow of doubt still troubling me. 'It's just, I thought you would have asked Duncan or something.'

Hannah sat down on her bed, holding a brown cuddly bear to her cheek. 'Yeah, I could have done I suppose. I just wanted someone who really cares about the play.'

'Oh . . . right.'

'Duncan's great and everything, but he said himself he'd rather be doing *West Side Story*.' She threw herself back on her pillow and started giggling. 'Did you see the way he started clicking his fingers in the fight scene?'

'It was pretty funny, wasn't it?' It was okay for Hannah to laugh at her own boyfriend, but I figured I'd better keep quiet about his tragic inability to speak poetry.

'But you, you're really good, Beth. I love what you're doing with the Nurse.'

'You do?'

'She's really caring and everything, but she's, like, so funny as well. That's why I want you to help me.'

The shadow of doubt had vanished completely. This was why I'd auditioned for the play in the first place. 'Of course I'll help you, Hannah. But you really don't need to worry about letting people down. You're perfect for Juliet. And I know for a fact that Mr Moore thinks you're amazing.'

'Thanks Beth,' she said, jumping up off the bed with a huge smile on her face. 'Perhaps we could have a go at Act Two Scene Five.'

'Sure. You might need to prompt me a bit though.'

'The audience is that way,' said Hannah, pointing at the rapper on the Cadillac and slipping into character in the blink of an eye. '*Oh God she comes! Oh honey Nurse, what news? Hast thou met him?*'

It was the part where the Nurse tells Juliet that Romeo wants to marry her in a secret ceremony at Friar Lawrence's cell. Fortunately this isn't a GCSE English lesson, but it's probably fair to say that if the Nurse hadn't encouraged a thirteen-year-old girl to sneak out of the house for underage sex with her parents' sworn enemy then the whole tragedy of Romeo and Juliet could easily have been averted.

But it was a lovely scene. The relationship between the old woman and the girl she'd cared for since birth was so trusting, so playful, so full of love; which was lucky because Hannah insisted on doing it about a million times. Mr Moore never tired of telling us that 'acting is about truth'. I guess that's why Hannah kept asking me if her performance felt 'real'.

It felt real all right. Even if I knew she was thinking about Duncan Fox. When I told her about Romeo's wedding plans, she flung her arms around my neck and kissed me. I wasn't sure if it was the Nurse who felt so happy for her, or just me.

It was probably a bit of both.

'Can we try it again?' said Hannah. 'That was okay, but I know I can do it better.'

'Okay, once more,' I said. 'But after that I want another biscuit.'

Hannah's energy was amazing. The scene was as fresh now as when we'd started. *'Oh God she comes! Oh honey Nurse, what —'*

But this time a new character burst into the scene. And he wasn't in the script. Nathan was standing in the doorway with a little red book in his hand and a huge grin on his face. 'Look what I've found.'

Hannah went white. 'What are you doing with my diary?'

'Shouldn't dump your bag in the kitchen, should you?'

'Have you been going through my things?'

'Maybe.'

'Nathan, I'm warning you. Give it here *now* or I'll smash your ugly little face in.'

He jumped onto her bed, waving the book in her face. 'Why should you care anyway? I thought you said I couldn't read.'

'I'm warning you.'

Nathan turned to a random page and started reciting. '*He's so . . . different from all the . . . others. He makes me feel* . . . Your writing's rubbish Hannah . . . *safe? Don't know if I love him but . . .*'

'Right that's it.'

'*. . . but when he . . . kissed me, I thought I was going to* . . . What's that say?'

Hannah grabbed his legs, bringing him down on the bed with a savage rugby tackle. And after she'd wrestled her diary back, she didn't let up, slapping him round the back of the head until he squealed for mercy. 'Don't ever ever *ever* take any of my stuff again.'

'I'm telling Mum,' said Nathan, fighting back the tears.

'She's not your mum anyway,' said Hannah. 'So stop calling her that.'

Nathan made a snivelling exit pursued by a (flying) bear. 'Cow!'

Hannah buried the diary under her pillow and threw herself on top. 'Pig! It's supposed to be private.'

'It's okay,' I said, half sympathetic, half wondering if she'd overreacted slightly. 'It was only me who heard. And I know who it's about anyway.'

'You do?'

'It's not exactly a secret, is it? Everyone knows you and Duncan are an item.'

This time she definitely overreacted, snapping back at me like I'd accused her of mass murder. 'Look, I'm not seeing anyone, okay?'

'Well, who was that you were writing about then?'

Hannah reached for a cuddly unicorn. 'Well . . . it *was* about Duncan . . . but I wrote it weeks ago.' At first she seemed hesitant but, after a moment, the whole sordid truth came flooding out. 'He's such a . . . kid. I dumped him after the first week of rehearsals. But he didn't want anyone to know. So he made me promise to pretend that we're still together until we finish the play.'

'And you agreed to that?'

'He was pretty upset. And it's only until the end of term.'

'That was *so* nice of you.'

She shrugged modestly.

'It must be hard though. Have you told any of your friends?'

'I wouldn't trust that lot,' said Hannah. 'Especially not AJ.'

'I thought you two were good friends.'

'Yeah, kind of. We've known each other since primary school. It's just that, these days, we don't seem to have much in common. I hate to say it, but she's actually a bit of a bitch.'

Little prickles of happiness were bristling up on the back of my neck. 'You know what, Hannah? If you want to keep a diary you should do it online. You can turn the settings to private so one else can read it.'

Hannah smiled. 'Good idea, I might just do that.'

I didn't tell her about the 'friends only' setting. Maybe that was something for another day.

'Night, Beth,' said Hannah's mum, handing me a sandwich bag full of Viennese Fingers. 'Hope to see you again sometime.'

'Doubt it,' said Hannah, 'not after all those questions. Anyway I'm going round Beth's on Thursday night. Isn't that right, Beth?'

It was what friends did; dreamed up on-the-spot alibis. There was probably something she didn't want her mum to know about. I'd seen it in the movies. Unfortunately I wasn't nearly as good at improvising as Hannah. 'Er . . . yes, that's . . . that's right. Perhaps Hannah could stay for something to eat.'

'Lovely,' said her mum. 'So long as it's all right with your parents.'

It was always a bit of a dilemma – whether to admit to a fifty per cent deficit in the parental department. Most of the time it was easier just to keep quiet.

'It'll be fine,' I said. 'They love meeting my friends.'

Hannah walked me to the door. 'Is that okay about Thursday?' she whispered. 'I really need to get out sometimes.'

I wish now that I'd tried to find out why. But I was far too excited to rock the boat. 'You mean you actually want to come then?'

'Is that a problem?'

'No, no . . . no, I just thought —'

'Great,' said Hannah. 'Maybe we could have lunch tomorrow, and talk about the play?'

'What about AJ and the others? Shakespeare's not exactly their thing, is it?'

'We could grab panninis and take them out to the Millennium Pagoda.'

I tried to look cool, but inside I was pumping my fist and letting out a sibilant *Yes!* 'Good idea, Hannah, that'd be nice.'

'And you won't tell anyone, will you? About Duncan I mean.'

'Course not,' I said, already racking my brains for that paralympian's pasta recipe. 'Don't worry Hannah, you can trust me.'

Waiting
for Hannah

As soon as the last bell went on Thursday, I started running. And I'd made it all the way to our 'special meeting place' before half the school had even got their chairs on the table. I couldn't believe she was actually coming to my house.

But a light sprinkling of rain was already dampening my spirits. I hadn't seen her since we crossed paths in the corridor before registration. Maybe Mr Catchpole still had her phone, because I'd texted about a million times and she hadn't replied. I needed to make sure she didn't have a nut allergy. Well that was my excuse anyway. I wanted to reassure myself she hadn't forgotten, which is why I'd spent half the day trying to track her down.

I'd thought we might be able to have lunch again. Yesterday was lovely. We'd talked more about our favourite movies than the play. But she wasn't in the canteen at second break, and by the time I'd tried the computer suite, the new drinks machine outside the Learning Resources Centre, the Millennium Pagoda and that place behind the temporary classrooms where the A-listers hung out, I was so desperate I even stuck my head round the door of the homework club.

And now she was twenty minutes late. Paranoia was stalking me with a rusty carving knife when a text pinged into my inbox: *Got held up. Meet at your house. What number is it?*

I texted back to ask if everything was okay.

Everything fine. See you asap. xx

Cooking alone always made me sad. I threw a handful of pine nuts into the saucepan and wondered if I'd got it all wrong. Hannah was certainly obsessed with acting; supposing she was just using me to practise her lines?

As soon as I opened the door, I knew that everything was going to be all right. Her hair was all over the place and her school jacket more crumpled than a flying carpet. But underneath, Hannah looked radiant. 'Nice house,' she said, dumping her soggy bag on the hall carpet. 'Sorry I'm late.'

'What happened?'

'Catchpole made me do detention. That bloke's got it in for me, I swear he has.'

'He can't do that, Hannah. He has to give you at least twenty-four hours' notice. You should tell your mum.'

'No,' said Hannah, emphatically. 'She'd tell Alan and

that would only make things worse.'

I hung her bag on the hooks by the front door and led her into the lounge. 'Why don't you sit by the fire, warm up a bit?'

'Wow, look at these books,' said Hannah, flopping down on the sofa. 'Have you read them all?'

'Not really,' I said. 'Most of them were my . . . Do you want a drink? I've got some Diet Coke in the fridge.' What the hell was I doing offering someone like Hannah Taylor soft drinks? 'Or maybe you'd like wine or something?'

'Don't worry, I'm fine thanks.'

'I've put out some olives. Help yourself.'

Hannah looked confused. 'I don't really . . . Are you supposed to eat them with these stick things?'

'Yeah,' I said, not sure if she was joking. 'I'll just go and boil the pasta. We'll have to eat first I'm afraid.'

'You didn't need to cook a meal or anything,' said Hannah. 'I just wanted to get out for a bit.'

'That's okay. I don't always eat properly when Dad's away. It'll do me good.'

I watched her through the serving hatch, just like I'd watched Mr Moore in his office. It gave me the same warm feeling inside, the same pangs of guilt about my voyeuristic tendencies. She went to the bookcase and pulled out *The Great Gatsby*, snooped round the photos on the mantelpiece and rearranged her hair in the mirror.

And then her phone went. Hannah laughed and started texting. Soon the messages were pinging back and forth, like a tennis match.

'Who was it?' I said, planting two bowls of tomato and pine-nut linguine on the coffee table.

'Just my mum,' said Hannah, slipping her phone back into her jacket pocket, 'checking up on me, as usual.'

'Oh right,' I said, trying not to feel jealous.

'This is . . . amazing,' said Hannah, picking at the linguine with her fork. 'I can't even make cheese on toast.'

'It's not that hard. You'd soon pick it up if you had to.'

'You're so lucky,' she said. 'Having the whole house to yourself.'

'You think so?'

'You've seen what it's like round ours,' said Hannah. 'Mum's on my case twenty-four seven, Nathan's a nightmare – and don't even get me started on Alan.'

I had no intention of doing that. 'The rehearsal went well yesterday, didn't it?'

'Yeah,' said Hannah, chasing a baby tomato round the pasta bowl. 'It's getting there.'

'I don't know how you do it. After everything that happened with Duncan, you still manage to make it look like you're madly in love.'

Hannah unleashed a tight smile.

'And Steve . . . I mean, Mr Moore, he liked our scene, didn't he?'

'Yeah,' she said. 'He seemed to.'

It wasn't the subtlest way of introducing the subject, but we were more or less officially friends by now, so it felt only right to share it with her. 'What do you think of him anyway – Mr Moore, I mean?'

Hannah speared an olive with a cocktail stick. 'He's okay, I guess.'

'I had a bit of a crush on him, actually.'

She crunched hard on a stone. 'Did you?'

'Well he's pretty . . . *hot*, isn't he?' It was probably the first time I'd ever used the word 'hot' in its traditional St Thomas's Community College context. Coming from my lips it sounded like a foreign language. (One that I wasn't fluent in, anyway.)

'I guess so,' said Hannah.

'In fact, you remember that love poem he did in Brighton?'

'What, "The Best Metaphors Are Taken"?'

'You're not going to believe this, but I actually convinced myself that he'd written it for me!'

Hannah looked genuinely shocked. 'You want to be careful, Beth.'

It was nice that she was looking out for me, but there was really no need. 'Don't worry. I'm not stupid. I'd never tell anyone – 'cept you of course. I mean *hello* – he's a teacher. He's got a wife and kid – well practically. People would think I was a right old . . . well, you know.'

Hannah pushed her pasta bowl away from her, balancing her fork on a pile of linguine. 'I didn't think you'd be bothered.'

'What?'

'You never seem to worry what people think about you. Like the way you're always hanging out with that George kid. You just don't care.'

'Yeah, well it's not quite . . .'

'That's what I like about you.'

And after M&S crème brûlée, Hannah asked me to help her with the scene where Juliet kills herself – the short passage in the tomb when she wakes up from the sleeping draught and finds Romeo dead.

'*O Happy dagger, this is thy sheath; there rust and let me die.*'

Her tears were certainly real enough; and the way she spoke the lines was just, well, heartbreaking. And I remembered what she'd said at the first rehearsal: *If you really loved someone, you couldn't live without them.* Back then it had sounded a bit far-fetched. But having seen Hannah in action, I was kind of warming to the idea.

She rose miraculously from the dead, dabbed her face with a tissue and joined me on the sofa.

'So you actually believe it then, Hannah? That Juliet would rather kill herself than live without Romeo?'

She didn't need to think twice. 'Yeah, course, don't you?'

But she was asking the wrong person. 'I don't know really. I've never been in love, have I?'

'Shame,' said Hannah. 'You don't know what you're missing.'

'Maybe not,' I said, suddenly deciding that I needed to tell her. 'But I do know what it feels like when a person you love . . . isn't there any more.'

'What do you mean?'

Almost 1,460 days later, I was finally going to tell someone from school. Grunt knew already, of course, but he was practically family so that didn't really count. 'I'm talking about my . . . I'm talking about my mum. Four years ago she . . .' And I almost said it; the horrible expression that everyone from the nurses at the hospice to that sweaty vicar seemed to think would make it sound better. *Don't say 'passed away', you idiots. I'm not stupid. She was my mum. And if I can say it, how come you lot are too pathetic to tell me she's DEAD.*

'Are you okay?' said Hannah, turning to face me again with an embarrassed smile.

'IdunnoifIcan . . .'

Hannah helped me out. 'Look, Beth, I know all about your mum dying . . . I think Duncan must have told me. Weren't you off school for a bit?'

'Yes . . . I didn't actually cope very well.'

'You were twelve years old!' said Hannah. 'My mum's, like, nearly fifty, but she cried for a week when Granddad died.'

There was so much I wanted to tell her: about the treatment that turned Mum's blue eyes yellow, about the techniques I developed to stop myself crying and the night before the funeral when none of them worked. But for now, the bare facts were enough. 'They told her she'd

107

beaten it – twice. And then one night she had this pain in her neck. About a year later she was dead.'

Hannah squirmed uneasily on the sofa. 'Look, I'm not being funny or anything. But why are you telling me this?'

'Because I never told anyone from school before.'

'You're kidding, right?'

'No. I tried to tell my friends, but I just couldn't. The more I wanted to, the harder it got. And then one day I realised I didn't have any friends any more.'

'So did she have a whatdoyoucallit . . . bucket list?'

'No. She sat where you are now, getting more and more depressed.'

Hannah squirmed even more uneasily. 'Well, did she leave you a letter or something – for after she was . . .?'

'No. She hardly ever talked about it; neither did Dad. In fact, he never really has.'

'You should talk to him,' said Hannah, firmly. 'I wish I'd talked to my dad when he was at home. If I try calling him now, he doesn't even pick up sometimes.'

'It's not that easy. Every time I mention her, he just walks away.'

She stared into my eyes like a teenage life coach. 'Then you'll have to make him listen.'

'How?'

'Tell him you don't want to forget her. Tell him she's part of you. Tell him that if you don't know your mother then you'll never really know yourself.'

Like I said, Hannah always seemed more mature

than the rest of us. It was as if *she'd* known me forever. 'I could give it a try I suppose.'

'It's like when I want to ask Mum for money,' she smiled. 'The important thing is picking the right moment.'

'Any day now ought to be good. It's almost exactly four years since she died. Trouble is, every time it's the same. February the eighteenth comes round and he just treats it like any other day.'

'And what about you?' said Hannah. 'What do *you* do?'

'Well…' Perhaps I'd spare her the details for now. It sounded pretty lame if you started analysing it. 'There is this kind of . . . ritual thing I do in the park – silly really.'

'And your dad doesn't know about it, right?'

'No,' I said, angry with him even as I said it. 'He'd only get all funny about it.'

'February the eighteenth. That's next week, isn't it?'

'Yes,' I said, wondering how it had crept up again so quickly. 'It wasn't actually my idea. But we spent a lot of time there, Mum and me – you know, feeding the ducks and that. And if *I* don't do something to remember her, no one else will.'

Hannah's eyes were clouding over. Not the millionairess pearls she cried over Romeo, but they looked real enough. 'That's really sad.'

'Don't worry about it,' I said, feeling a strange urge to cheer her up. 'This year's been way better already.'

'Why's that?'

'Oh . . . you know, doing the play and everything. It's been great, hasn't it?'

'Yes, yes it has,' said Hannah.

And I was about to say that our fledgling friendship was probably the best thing that had happened to me since my mum died when Hannah's phone went.

She smiled and tapped back a text. 'That was my mum. She's parked round the corner. I'd better go.'

'Oh right,' I said, struggling hard to hide my disappointment. 'Well, thanks for coming and . . . maybe we could do it again one night.'

'Yeah sure,' said Hannah, glancing at her mobile. 'If you'd like to.'

'Are you kidding?' I said, failing miserably to suppress my inner stalker. 'You're like the dream friend.'

Hannah blushed modestly. 'You know what, Beth? Maybe you don't know me as well as you think.'

'What do you mean?'

'Nothing . . . nothing. I don't deserve the compliment, that's all.' And suddenly she was smiling. 'Look, I tell you what, why don't I come with you next week, to the park. I mean, for your mum's memorial thingy. That's if you'd like me to.'

'Of course I would. That would be amazing.'

'Good,' said Hannah. 'You'd better text me the details.'

'I usually go down there after school. But seeing as it's half term, we could meet in town first if you like.'

'Yeah . . . I mean, I'd like to, but I'm pretty busy next

110

week. So I'd probably better give town a miss.'

'Yeah . . . course.'

'But I'll meet you in the park on Thursday afternoon, promise.'

'Great.'

'And try and talk to your dad, yeah?'

'I will do. And thanks for being such a —'

'Look, sorry Beth, my mum goes mental if I keep her waiting. I have to go.'

When we reached the door, I thought she was going to hug me. The other girls started doing it in Year Nine. It was another St Thomas's tradition I'd somehow managed to avoid.

'Thanks for a great night,' she said, sidestepping my tentatively outstretched arms and grabbing her bag from the hook. 'I'll see you next week then.'

'What about at school tomorrow?'

'I won't be there,' she said, straightening her collar. 'I've got this . . . funeral; no one close or anything. But Mum's still making me go.'

'I'll miss you,' I said, feeling like a total idiot the moment I'd said it. 'I mean, take care and I'll see you next week.'

Dad had fitted a whole new security system. I activated the burglar alarm and fastened the Mr Scrooge locks and chains before hurrying back to the lounge, hoping to catch a glimpse of Hannah and her mum. But by the time I peeped through the curtains, they were gone.

Unlikely Couples
& Serial Killers

You've probably guessed by now that we're not heading for a Hollywood ending here. So it's hardly a spoiler when I say that *Le Grand Meaulnes* had about as much chance of a 'happy ever after' as I did. Perhaps the clue was in the blurb: *The search for an unobtainable love.* But that didn't stop me spending the first few days of half term hoping that Augustin Meaulnes (our eponymous anti-hero) would somehow get it together with his mystery girl.

Mum worked as a translator; French crime novels mainly and the occasional holiday romance. She was always complaining about unlikely couples and even more unlikely serial killers, so I think she'd have been pleased that I was into the classics. They were a good way of avoiding Dad. I'd tried talking to him, like

Hannah suggested, but his annual festival of denial was in full swing. The bogus cheeriness and 'comedy' French accent were far easier to ignore with your head in a book.

Mum would have been happy that I'd found a new friend too, even if Hannah's diary was fuller than the Queen's. When she wasn't babysitting the dreaded Nathan or indoor snowboarding with her dad in Milton Keynes, she was reinstalling iTunes or revising for the mocks. But at least she returned my texts. And by the time Thursday came, I was half looking forward to it. Sharing the moment with Hannah would make the whole thing more bearable.

Plus which, I really needed some time away from Dad. It was only February, but he'd embarked on a feverish bout of spring cleaning, turning out the cupboards in the spare room and swearing like a panellist on a comedy quiz show.

'What are you looking for?' I said, popping my head round the door and peering at the carnage.

'Nothing,' said Dad defensively. 'Why is this place such a mess?'

'I'm just off out then,' I said, making a dash for the stairs.

'*Au revoir*,' called Dad, miraculously recovering his faux *joie de vivre* by the time I reached for my coat.

As usual, I stopped at the party shop to pick up supplies. I had a funny feeling the woman with the axe through her head remembered me from last year. This

113

time I bought a balloon for Hannah too, trailing them across town like a Year Seven girl on her birthday.

The weather was appropriately grim – grey and spitting rain. No wonder the pond was deserted. The gate had an advert for the sponsored cancer walk that Dad refused to take me on. I pushed it open and went inside. I'd loved that place when I was a kid. Mum took stale bread for the ducks. But you weren't supposed to feed them any more, and it was crawling with rat traps. It smelled funny too. The bench beneath the weeping willow was so smothered in bird poo that you had to squeeze up to the armrest and hope for the best.

I was getting used to Hannah being late. But by four o'clock I'd started to panic. Every time I called her I went straight through to voicemail. The fact that her house was only ten minutes' walk away only made things worse. How much longer should I wait?

And when staring into the scummy water and doing battle with the gag reflex lost its glamour, I closed my eyes and tried to picture Mum. It was getting harder. There were several reminders dotted about the house but most of them were from the days before I knew her: a serious looking graduation photo, a silly one with Uncle Simon wearing Spock ears, and a windswept wedding. I could just about remember her blue-eyed smile, but now when I thought about her, my main impression was of a kind of warm-towelled 'mumness' (or do I mean numbness?) that left me happy and desolate at the same time.

And I was trying hard to conjure up her pre-chemo hair (shoulder length with blond highlights) when a high-pitched voice, like one of the Chipmunks, dragged me back to reality.

'Hi Beth. How are you doing?'

'Oh, it's you.'

The camouflage jacket and Bob Marley T-shirt were a dead giveaway. He stepped out of the bushes, still struggling to re-tie his balloon. Believe it or not, the helium-voice thing actually used to make me laugh. When he spoke again, he was back to his croaky normal. 'I thought I'd find you here.'

It hadn't crossed my mind that he'd turn up as usual. Considering the way I'd been treating him, it was actually pretty amazing. 'Yeah, well.'

Grunt obviously didn't care about the bird poo. He sat down beside me, his red balloon hovering above us at the end of its string. 'Are you expecting someone?'

'What?'

'You've got two balloons. I just thought . . .'

I could have lied and said that one was for him. But we'd hardly spoken since I started hanging out with Hannah. 'Hannah said she might come down, but it looks like she's . . .'

'Right,' nodded Grunt. 'Bummer.'

'She probably had to stay at her dad's or something – in Milton Keynes.'

'Yeah . . . probably.'

It was all Grunt's idea, the thing in the park: *We could*

do it every year. Your mum liked balloons – remember that game we played on Boxing Day? And she loved *Arthur. It* *was her favourite cartoon. I reckon it's the perfect way to* *remember her.* Back in Year Seven, it was a miracle if he spoke more than a couple of sentences, but he was the only one who didn't act like it had never happened.

'Thanks for coming,' I said, shooting a last hopeful glance across the park towards the Sports Centre. 'Sorry about the weather.'

'No worries.'

'And I'm sorry if I've been a bit . . .'

Grunt reached self-consciously for his epaulets. 'Are we going to do this or not?'

'Yeah, let's do it.'

We walked down to the water's edge, the hungry ducks quacking at our ankles. It was kind of embarrassing that we still knew the words to the *Arthur* theme tune, so we started in a tuneless whisper and only really went for it when we got to the chorus. But by the time we released three red balloons into the wild, they could probably hear us in the skateboard park.

The wind caught the first one, marooning it on a holly bush where it withered and died. The other two floated up into the cold grey sky.

'I still miss her you know,' said Grunt, squinting at the clouds. 'Remember those cupcakes with the pink icing?'

'Yes,' I said, not daring to admit that I could barely remember her face.

'She was all right, your mum.'

'Yeah.'

Since when had Grunt started wearing hair gel? He slid back his palm across the top of his head and wiped it on Bob Marley. 'Do you want to go into town? We could look round the charity shops for vinyl or something.'

'I'd better wait for Hannah.'

'What's the matter with you?' said Grunt, his anger clearly visible now despite the camouflage jacket. 'She's not coming, Beth. I told you about her before.'

'Hannah's not like that.'

'So where is she then?'

'I don't know. Maybe . . .'

'Look, I don't know what she's playing at, but she's using you for something, I know she is. Come on, Beth. Let's go into town.'

Hannah was over half an hour late. She hadn't made the slightest effort to contact me and, let's face it, it wasn't the first time. Maybe Grunt was right. 'Okay then. But there's no way I'm looking for smelly old records. We could get a drink if you like.'

'Great, let's . . .' Grunt's smile seemed to fade to black, like one of his spotlights.

My face did exactly the opposite.

Hannah was legging it across the football pitches, deftly avoiding the mini footballers and their mums, still managing to look gorgeous in her green woolly tights. She flung open the gate and pulled up in front of us with an apologetic smile. 'Have I missed anything?'

'Yes, you have actually,' said Grunt. 'Beth couldn't wait any longer.'

'Sorry, sorry . . . *sorry*,' she puffed. 'I got held up, that's all.'

But I'd already forgiven her. 'That's okay. Don't worry about it.'

Grunt definitely hadn't. 'Unbelievable.'

'Couldn't we do it again or something?' said Hannah.

Grunt's face hardened, like quick-drying cement. 'No we could not. Me and Beth are going into town, aren't we, Beth?'

'Look, I'm really sorry, but I think I'd better stay with Hannah.'

'Right, that's it, I'm off,' said Grunt, turning at the gate to fire his parting shot. 'She's not your friend, all right? And just remember, Beth – you heard it here first.'

'Wait,' I called. 'Maybe we could all go together.' But he was already stumbling through the football match, trying – as he always had done – to avoid the ball.

'Why don't you go after him?' said Hannah.

'It's all right, he'll calm down in a minute. I'm just so glad you could make it.'

'Told you I would, didn't I?'

And we were halfway to the Park Café before I dared ask. 'So what kept you?'

'I told you, I got held up, that's all.'

'Yes, but by what? Nothing to do with Alan was it?'

Hannah stared down at her purple Doc Martens, fingers twitching at her sides. '*No* . . . it was just, you

118

know . . . stuff. Anyway, what have *you* been up to? Are you all set for the run-through next week?'

I knew something was wrong. And I had a strong feeling her stepfather was involved. I'd never met Alan, but it was pretty obvious she was hiding something. So why did I let her seduce me with a twitter of small talk? Simple really: because even to a passing jogger, we must have looked like really close mates. How shallow was that?

If I was any kind of friend I'd have kept pestering her until she'd told me everything. No wonder I felt so ashamed of myself. In fact, I was almost relieved when her phone went and she said she'd have to go.

'Mum wants me to look after Nathan. I'll see you on Monday, yeah?'

In fact, it was rather sooner than that.

How to Look
Ten Years Younger

Dad was up in the attic. He'd been tearing the house apart since he got back from Bangkok.

'What are you *doing* up there?'

'Looking for something.' His voice echoed like a character in a horror movie. 'Oh bugger!'

'If you tell me what you're looking for, I might be able to help.'

There was someone at the door. It was hard to imagine what life would be like if Mum hadn't died, although I was pretty certain she wouldn't have tolerated Dad's deafening new door chimes.

'Get that will you, Beth?'

The bell never went on Sunday afternoons. In fact, it hardly went at all. Our only regular visitors were blokes selling expensive dusters, assorted pizza people and

120

Grunt – but he hadn't called in a while.

Just for a moment, I really didn't know who it was; which considering I'd spent most of the weekend thinking about her, shows you how terrible she looked. It was as if someone had melted wax crayons over her face: a startling mixture of blue, pink and orange topped with a spider's web of mascara. And to make the whole effect more random, she was wearing a strapless red dress that left little to the imagination unless it was trying to figure out why on earth she was wearing it in the first place.

'Hannah, what happened to you?'

'Can I come in, please?' she whispered between sobs.

'Yeah, course,' I said, ushering her through the doorway and giving her a prototype Year Nine hug, which she didn't resist. 'Are you all right? Do you want me to call your mum?'

She squeezed my arm just a little too tightly. '*No*. I don't want to talk to her, I'm . . .'

My comforting arm on her shoulder failed miserably to stem the tears. 'Okay, fine, so why don't you talk to *me*. What is it, Hannah? Why are you so upset?'

'I didn't know where else to come.'

Despite her misery, I couldn't help feeling a tiny bit elated. 'Do you want the bathroom? There's one under the stairs.'

She was in the loo forever. Where she could have hidden it in that dress was anyone's guess, but I had a feeling she was using her phone; every now and then what sounded like the ping of a text rose above her sobbing.

She looked about ten years younger without make-up. It was certainly an improvement on the pitiful creature who'd walked in. 'How do you feel now?' I said.

'Fine,' said Hannah. But I knew she was lying.

Dad had abandoned his search in the attic. Even without eyeliner, Hannah had a magical effect on him. The mood he'd been in all weekend lifted instantly. 'Hello there. I remember you. It's Hannah, isn't it?'

She very nearly managed a smile. 'That's right.'

'I hope Beth's looking after you. Has she offered you a drink?'

'We're going up to my room,' I said, grabbing Hannah and steering her away from him. 'We want to practise some scenes from the play.'

'Ah yes, this famous play,' said Dad. 'Which part are you, Hannah?'

'Juliet.'

'Of course you are,' said Dad, draping an arm round the bottom of the banisters. 'I used to do a bit of acting myself.'

'Come on,' I said. 'Let's go upstairs.'

Hannah sat on the bed, shivering. I sat beside her, wishing I could think of something consoling to say.

'Nice room,' she eventually sniffed. 'I like the poster.'

'And I . . . really like your outfit,' I said, mainly to avoid another difficult silence, because to be totally honest, I thought it looked a bit tacky.

'It's my prom dress,' said Hannah. 'We got it in the sales.'

'Right, and er . . . why did you decide to wear it today?'

'I was . . . trying it on,' she said, shivering uncontrollably, but still not explaining why she'd decided to run all the way to my house in her prom dress.

'You look freezing. Why don't you borrow something of mine?' I went to the wardrobe and slid open the doors. According to Dad they were all designer labels. For all I knew they could have been. 'There must be something in here.'

'Whoa,' said Hannah. 'Where did you get all that?'

'Dad always brings me back something when he goes away. Here – what about this?' I took out a chunky mohair cardigan and wrapped it round her shoulders.

'It's lovely,' she said.

'Keep it if you like. I never wear half this stuff.'

For some reason that started Hannah off again; her teary honesty was just how I imagined the end of a Year Ten party. 'You know what Beth, you're actually really nice. I don't think you're up yourself at all.'

'Is that what they all think of me?'

'Well, maybe a few of them,' said Hannah, tactfully. 'But not me, I think you're great.'

'Thanks.'

'You don't think I'm a bad person, do you, Beth?'

'Of *course* not. Where did that come from?'

Hannah hesitated, grabbing a handful of duvet in her small white fist. 'There's something I need to talk about.'

'What is it?'

'First you've got to swear not to tell anyone.' There was a hardness in her voice that hadn't been there before. 'I will *never* forgive you if you do.'

'Okay, fine.'

'Well go on then, swear.'

I had the feeling that if a Bible had been available she'd definitely have made me use it. 'Okay . . . I swear.'

Hannah was wavering. 'He made me promise to keep it a secret,' she whispered. 'He said it was the only way.'

It looked like my suspicions were well founded. 'Is this about your stepfather, Hannah? Is that what you need to talk about?'

She didn't speak, but I could see the fear in her eyes. 'No, no it's nothing I . . .'

'Look, I can't do anything about it if you won't tell me.'

Hannah took a deep breath. 'Well you see, I've been —'

Seven jaunty knocks later, Dad popped his head round my bedroom door. 'I thought you might like to see what I found in the attic. It's my old school magazine. That's me in *The Importance of Being Earnest*.'

Why was he wearing a dress? I don't think that's what frightened Hannah off, but Dad's entrance was certainly her cue for a swift exit. 'Sorry, sorry,' she said, pushing past him and out into the hall, 'I've got to go, I'll see you later.'

'Don't let me drive you away,' said Dad.

But Hannah was already halfway down the stairs. I raced her to the front door, like an overenthusiastic hostess. 'Hannah, wait. What's up? What is it that you won't tell me?'

'Nothing . . . it's nothing. Please, Beth, just forget it, yeah?'

'I don't know if I can.'

Hannah wrenched open the door, checking first that Dad wasn't listening before turning to face me with a vicious glare. 'Look, if you're any kind of a friend you'll keep your mouth shut.'

'Please, just tell me.'

'I can't,' she said, disappearing into the cold, grey afternoon.

'Hannah, *please*,' I called. 'It might seem bad now, but I'm sure it's not as bad as you think.'

O Woeful, Woeful, Woeful Day

The next time I saw her – on Monday morning in Drama – she was all smiles. But Hannah wasn't fooling anyone. She was just a great actress. How else could she have managed to look so fascinated by Mr Moore's lesson on Bertolt Brecht?

And afterwards when I caught up with her in the corridor, she tried to turn Sunday night into a 'funny' story. 'I was getting my period, that's all. You know how it is; sometimes I'm all over the place.'

'Why did you run off like that?' I said, trying to keep up with her as she sped out to the courtyard. 'Come on, Hannah, I'm worried about you.'

'Everything's fine.'

Maybe she didn't want to talk about it at school. 'Do you want to come round mine tonight? We could get a takeaway.'

'I can't, sorry. I'm doing something.'

'What about tomorrow?'

Hannah stepped up the pace. 'No, don't think so.'

I was practically running by now. 'Why were you crying like that?'

'I told you, it was nothing.'

'Hannah *please*, I'm your friend. I just want to help, that's all.'

She obviously didn't see it that way. 'Look, if you really want to help, you'll keep your mouth shut, okay?'

Hannah avoided me for the rest of the week. Even at rehearsals, she found a way of restricting our off-stage dialogue to a couple of sentences. Of course, I forgave her; whatever her problem, she was so wrapped up in it that she didn't have time for anything else.

But I didn't want to let her down. She needed me more than ever now. It was just a case of doing the right thing. But what was that exactly? My first instinct was to report my suspicions to a responsible adult. Mr Moore was the obvious choice. Unlike Mr Catchpole, he wouldn't convene a committee, and he knew Hannah pretty well. Several times I stood outside his open door, but she'd sworn me to secrecy and I was determined to be the kind of friend she could trust.

But sooner or later I'd have to broach the subject again. Knowing Hannah, she was nervous about the run-through on Friday. Once that was out of the way, maybe she'd be ready to talk.

* * *

The warm-up was over. Mr Moore stood in front of a half
painted version of Brighton seafront, shielding his eyes
from Grunt's glaring spotlights. 'Okay guys, this is it – our
first run-through. I just wanted to say, I'm very excited
about tonight, because you lot have been amazing.'

'So have you, sir,' called one of his Year Eight admirers.

'I love you, Mr Moore!' squealed Pete Hughes,
slicking back his hair with a plastic flick knife.

Mr Moore joined in with the laughter. He looked
really happy that night. 'Thank you, Chantelle, that's
very kind of you.' His eyes were twinkling and it really
felt like he believed in us. 'Now, if you only remember
one thing tonight, it's this . . .'

Everyone in the cast chanted it back to him, like
theatrical zombies. '*Acting is about truth!*'

'Exactly,' smiled Mr Moore. 'Now as you know,
Mr Edmonds was worried that a St Thomas's audience
couldn't cope with a full-length Shakespeare.'

'Philistines,' muttered Dave Denyer.

[Just to digress for a moment, there's another story
that I'd probably touch upon if I had more time. It may
not be as sensational as some of the stuff that's coming
later, but it was, in its way, just as amazing. Whoever
could have predicted that Dave Denyer would discover
a lifelong love of Shakespeare? He seemed to have a real
eye for the 'stage picture', and by the time we got to the
dress rehearsal he was even offering advice on speaking
blank verse.]

'And I've promised we can keep the show under two hours. So please, please, *please*, pick up those cues.'

Miss Hoolyhan was tuning a banjo. Unlike Mr Moore, she looked pretty miserable. In fact, she'd been a bit off with us since the night of the poetry gig. 'And for pity's sake, speak up. I'm going to be prompting, and it's no good if I can't hear you. Oh and skiffle band, it's B flat, all right? Don't make me remind you again.'

Grunt was sitting in the front row with the lighting desk on his lap. 'We haven't quite finished plotting the LX yet,' said Mr Moore, 'so if you find yourself in darkness, keep calm and carry on acting.'

Dave Denyer jumped onto the miniature version of Brighton Pier that doubled as a balcony. 'Right, Montagues and Capulets – I don't want any pissing about. This is street fighting, not origami. If you're going to kick someone in the head, do it like you mean it. Like Steve says, acting's all about truth.' You could see that underneath he was bursting with pride. 'Anyway . . . cheers for . . . You've got something really special here. Don't mess it up.'

'Okay everyone, that's your five minute call,' said Mr Moore, taking a seat next to Grunt and opening his reporter's notebook. 'If you want to sit out front when you're not performing that's fine by me, just make sure you don't miss your entrances. And one more thing: it's really not the end of the world if something goes wrong tonight. We've got two whole weeks to fix it.'

* * *

The skiffle band was slowly strangling 'A Teenager in Love'. Grunt dimmed the lights, leaving only a tight circle at the front of the stage. A startled Year Eight stepped into it, tugged at his trouser leg and cleared his throat:

'*Two households both alike in dignity in fair . . . in fair . . .*'

'*Verona,*' hissed Miss Hoolyhan.

Behind the scenes, the excitement was so tangible you could cut it with a plastic flick knife. Kids who hardly said two words to each other in normal school were hugging like long lost friends, swept along on a tsunami of hysterical optimism.

Hannah was standing by the props table, waiting for her first entrance. I'd planned to keep out of her way until afterwards, but I wanted her to know that she wasn't alone.

'Good luck,' I whispered. 'You're going to be brilliant.'

A gleam of friendly recognition flickered across her face. 'Fingers crossed, eh?' And a moment later, she was gone.

I'm not pretending it was the greatest production of *Romeo and Juliet* in the world, but I like to think it could have been good. The fight scenes looked genuinely life-threatening, Pete Hughes's Mercutio was laugh-out-loud funny (although not always in the right places) and Duncan Fox made an okay-ish Romeo once you got used to all that strutting about.

Even more impressive was the way the whole cast

pulled together. The sarcastic running commentary that formed the backdrop to virtually every activity at St Thomas's was miraculously absent. That was down to Mr Moore. His enthusiasm was like the Black Death; we all caught it in the end. If he said your scene was 'sensational', you just believed him.

But it was only when Hannah stepped onto the stage that the performance really came alive. She *was* Juliet. Every word, every sigh, every tiny gesture made you believe that this funny, beautiful, slightly wilful teenager had fallen in love. And after all that extra rehearsing together, our scenes flowed so naturally I hardly felt nervous at all.

That's how I like to remember Hannah Taylor. Not for what happened later, but for how she was in that first run-through. Once I'd made my final exit, I crept out front to watch her in the last act. Even the Year Eights sat engrossed as Juliet woke up alongside her dead husband, realising instantly that life without him was unthinkable.

'Oh happy dagger, this is thy sheath.'

Mr Moore stopped scribbling notes; Grunt looked up from his lighting desk; Miss Hoolyhan was in tears – if anyone forgot their lines they were in big trouble. But the concentration was so fierce by now that the end of the play seemed to act itself.

Dave Denyer led the applause as the skiffle band launched into 'Stupid Cupid'.

Mr Moore jumped to his feet and punched the air.

'That was absolutely phenomenal. You guys should be proud of yourselves. Unfortunately we seem to have overrun a bit, so we'll give you your notes on Monday. Have a great weekend now. You deserve it.'

We swarmed, euphoric, into the night, Pete Hughes reprising the Queen Mab speech in an Australian accent and an impromptu choir blasting out 'A Teenager in Love'. The last time I'd seen Hannah, she was returning her bloody dagger to the props table. But she'd disappeared in the mad scramble for the door.

A herd of grey people-carriers was lined up in the car park. Like me, Hannah wasn't the kind of girl whose parents insisted on a door-to-door delivery service, but I checked the windscreens just in case.

She wasn't at the bus stop either. What if she was still avoiding me? I cast a nostalgic glance at our 'special meeting place' under the tree. Maybe I should text her tomorrow morning. She'd be far more likely to talk to me if I arranged to meet her alone.

'Hey Beth, wait up.' Grunt was snapping at my heels, the ghost of a Snickers Bar still haunting his lips. 'Well done tonight. You were loads better than I expected.'

'Thanks a lot.'

'And your . . . friend, Hannah. She was scarily good.'

'What do you mean?'

'All that crying. And topping herself and stuff. No offence, Beth, but everyone else looks like they're just pretending. With her, it's like she's actually doing it for real. It's not natural, is it?'

Grunt rarely speculated on his fellow pupils' emotional states. That's why it hit me so hard; the pang of conscience that brought me to my senses and made me turn back towards the school. 'Sorry, I think I left something in the drama studio. I'd better go and find it.'

'That's okay. I'll come with you.'

'No, please. I need to go on my own.'

Grunt's shoulders seemed to fold around his head. 'Oh, right, I get it.'

The lights were going out all over the school. Exhausted cleaners were trooping across the courtyard in their bright blue sweatshirts and the uncharacteristically cheerful figure of Mr Catchpole was heading home at last, swinging his Tesco bag and whistling classical music.

At least the drama studio was still open. It was dark onstage, but a shaft of light was spilling from Mr Moore's office at the back, creating a pier-shaped shadow on the floor. Thank goodness he was still there. I had to tell him about Hannah. Maybe it was nothing. But whatever I might have promised, I'd never forgive myself if she got hurt.

I stumbled towards the light, picking my way through Grunt's tangled web of cables, suddenly aware of muffled laughter. Perhaps Mr Moore was trying to cheer up Miss Hoolyhan. She certainly looked like she needed it these days. It would probably be easier to talk to both of them anyway; I still got a bit 'flustered' in his presence.

I paused for a moment to rehearse my speech: *I'm very worried about Hannah Taylor. I think someone might be . . . It's Hannah, I've got this terrible feeling . . . I hope you don't think I'm being silly but . . .*

The laughter stopped as I approached the open door.

Looking into his office, I saw exactly why.

But although I turned away in disgust, it was too late. The sickening image was burned onto my retina for the rest of time: eyes closed and joined at the mouth, they clung to each other, like some monstrous blind beast.

And before I ran, I forced myself to look again. There was a million to one chance that I'd got it wrong. What if the girl he was kissing, the girl with her arms wrapped tightly round his neck, who looked exactly like her and had the same spidery ladder in the back of her tights . . . What if it wasn't Hannah at all?

ACT FOUR

Smiling
& Texting

'You do know what time it is?'

I'd been awake all night trying to get my head around it. There were so many questions that needed answering. When did it all start? How on earth had they managed to keep it a secret? And was I the dumbest person in the universe for not suspecting a thing? She was lucky I'd managed to contain myself for so long.

'I need to talk to Hannah.'

Steph Poole yawned and rearranged her stripy pyjama bottoms. 'I normally let her lie in on Saturday mornings.'

'It's important,' I said.

'Something to do with the play, is it?'

'You could say that.'

'Well all right then,' she said, reluctantly ushering me across the *Welcome* mat. 'But no one's up yet; apart from

Nathan, of course.'

'Can I just see her, please?'

'Right, yes . . . er, would you like a cup of tea first?'

'No.'

Steph Poole looked confused. Was this the same girl who'd gone into polite ecstasies over her Viennese Fingers?

'You know where it is, don't you?' She stood at the bottom of the stairs and hollered. 'Hannah . . . wake up, Hannah, there's someone to see you. All right, Beth, you'd better —'

I thundered up the stairs, still not sure who I was most angry with. Hannah and Mr Moore were right up there but, most of all, I was furious with myself. How could I have been so stupid?

Nathan was sitting at the top of the stairs, zapping 3D aliens. 'What's the password?'

'Look, I haven't got time for this.'

'You can't come through without the password.'

'I have to see Hannah.'

'Hannah's an idiot,' said Nathan.

'You can say that again.'

This seemed to please him. 'It's bum hole. The password is bum hole. Say that and you can come through.'

'Get stuffed, Nathan,' I said, allowing myself the added pleasure of whacking him round the head as I pushed past.

'You can't do that.'

'Well that's funny, I think I just did.'

I burst through her door like a TV cop on a drugs raid. Hannah was sitting up in bed, wearing a Princess Fiona T-shirt and a self-satisfied smile, texting at the speed of light. 'Hi Beth, what are you —'

'Don't give me any of that "Hi Beth" crap.'

She was still smiling and texting. 'What are you talking about?'

'You must think I'm a complete idiot.'

'Course I don't,' she said, her smile morphing instantaneously from self-satisfied to terminally patronising. 'Everyone knows you're one of the cleverest kids in the school.'

'Don't do that.'

'Do what?'

'You *know* what.'

Hannah looked confused. Was this the same girl who'd followed her round the school like a lovesick Labrador? 'Do you want to come in again, babe? I think we got off on the wrong foot, don't you? And shut the door behind you. We don't want that brat Nathan listening, do we?'

'Got something to hide, have you?' I said, shutting it anyway.

'What's all this about?'

It was time to come to the point. 'Who are you texting, Hannah?'

'Just . . . someone.'

She'd made me suffer. Now it was time to repay the

compliment. 'Oh yeah . . . like who?'

'Duncan . . . Duncan, it's Duncan,' she said, tapping out a final sentence before turning off her phone. 'He keeps texting me. It's doing my head in.'

'Oh yes, Duncan, you're so-called ex. The one you have this cosy little arrangement with. God, Hannah, you're *sooo* nice.'

Her smile had all but vanished. 'If you've got something to say, Beth, why don't you say it?'

'I know what happened last night.'

'What are you on about?'

My anger had burned itself out. All I wanted now was to get it over with. 'How long has it been going on?'

'What?'

'Do you want me to draw you a picture?'

'It's a bit early for Pictionary, isn't it?'

The room started swaying. I sank onto the pink beanbag at the side of her bed. 'I was so worried. I thought your stepfather might be . . . you know . . . hurting you . . .'

Hannah seemed to find this very funny. 'Oh my God, you didn't? Alan's a total dickhead, but he'd never do anything like that.'

'Yes, I know that now. But I didn't last night. That's when I decided to tell someone.'

You could see her brain ticking over. 'Why would you do that?'

'I thought we were friends. I thought that's what friends did.'

140

'I told you to keep your mouth shut,' snapped Hannah.

'Yes, and now I know why. After the rehearsal I went back to find Mr Moore. I thought it would be better if I told someone who knew you. Only I didn't realise quite how well until I saw you together in his office.'

'Oh . . . yeah . . . that's right. I . . . *did* go back to his office. He said he wanted to give me a couple of notes so I could think about them over the weekend.'

She was a great actress, but she wasn't that good. 'Stop it, just stop it. I saw exactly what you were doing. Don't lie to me, Hannah. How long has this been going on?'

She peeled back the duvet and swung her legs onto the floor. 'How long has what been going on?'

'I saw you, Hannah. Don't try and deny it. Come on, how long?'

At last, the lying stopped. 'Since that night in Brighton,' she said. 'Well, maybe a bit before.'

And suddenly everything became clearer. 'All those times you were late; you were seeing him, weren't you? I was just a convenient alibi, wasn't I?'

'No Beth, it wasn't like that . . . really.'

'Okay then, so tell me what it *was* like.'

'It started out as a bit of fun. I'd go to his room after school, and he'd play me his favourite songs and stuff. It wasn't until after Brighton that our relationship started getting serious.'

'Just listen to yourself, Hannah. Relationship? It's not a "relationship", it's just, well, *wrong*. How could he do that?'

141

'It's not just him, you know. I know what I'm doing.'

She really didn't get it. 'You're a kid and he's a teacher. It's up to him to do the right thing. He'll lose his job and everything. You know that, don't you?'

'I won't tell anyone if you don't. Oh come on, Beth. You said yourself you fancied him.'

'Yeah, but I would *never* have . . . acted on it.' Why was I blushing when I knew it was true? 'How far has it gone anyway?'

Her silence seemed to say it all.

'He's got a wife and baby, Hannah. What's he playing at?'

'That doesn't mean anything,' she said. 'The baby's dead sweet and that, but Archie's the only reason he stays with her.'

'That's what he says anyway.'

'It's true. Me and Steve love each other.' The terrible thing is, I really think she believed it.

'Love? You don't know the meaning of the word, Hannah. If he gave a flying toss about you, he would never have done something so stupid.'

'What would you know anyway?' she said, tears of defiance slithering down her cheeks. 'You're just jealous.'

'You realise I'm going to have to report him.'

At first she tried to look like she didn't care. 'Go ahead then. No one will believe you.'

'I saw you kissing him. I think they take that kind of thing pretty seriously these days.'

'You'd never do it anyway.'

But when I struggled out of the beanbag and made for the door, she grabbed my arm and started begging. 'Beth, no . . . please . . . don't. Like you said, he'll lose his job. He'll lose everything. It's not his fault anyway. I was the one who started it.'

'I doubt that very much. And anyway, it doesn't matter who started it. He should never have let it happen in the first place.'

'You can't help who you fall in love with, Beth. He's a good teacher too. You know that.'

'Yes but —'

'And nothing's really happened. Only what you saw.'

I really wanted to believe her. 'Honestly?'

'I swear on my mother's life. Please, Beth, promise me you won't say anything.'

If I've learned anything in the last year, it's that people will do the stupidest things in the name of love. I've also learned that one of the strongest versions out there is the love you feel for a friend. I wasn't sure what she felt for me any more, but I didn't want to lose her. And right at that moment, a friend was exactly what she needed. After everything that had happened, I still wanted to please her.

'All right. But you've got to finish it.'

It was like someone had plunged a knife into her stomach, the way she clutched herself in pain. 'No, no, I can't. We tried breaking up, but it was just too hard. That's why I was in such a state when I came to your house.'

'This isn't Walt Disney, Hannah. Trust me, whatever

happens here, there's not going to be a happy ending. Either you tell him it's over or I'm going straight to Mr Edmonds.'

She closed her eyes, like she was praying. I just hoped God saw it the same way as I did. And finally she spoke. 'Okay, I'll do it.'

'So you'll tell him then?'

'Yeah, I'll tell him this afternoon. We're supposed to be going to Brighton.'

'Are you sure that's a good idea? Can't you just text him?'

'No,' she said, throwing herself back on the bed and kind of shouting into her pillow. 'What's the matter with you? If I have to break up with him, the least I can do is say it to his face.'

'Okay, okay, but after that you've got to stay away from him.'

'What about the play?'

I hadn't thought of that. 'Make sure there's always someone with you. I can always help with that if you like.'

I knew she was crying again. The back of her shoulders were twitching. 'It's for the best, Hannah, really it is. I know you feel terrible now, but you're doing the right thing, I promise.'

'You think so?' she whispered.

'Of course.' There was one last question that I hardly dared ask. 'Maybe we could get together sometime next week. What do you think?'

'Eh?'

'I mean, we can still be friends, can't we? It doesn't mean that . . .'

'Yeah . . . sure,' she said, turning back towards me, her tears finally under control. 'But you've got to promise me one thing. You can't tell anyone about Steve and me. Please, I need to know I can trust you.'

I nodded stiffly. 'Call me as soon as you've told him.'

At about four o clock that afternoon when she still hadn't contacted me, I started leaving her messages: 'Have you done it yet?'; 'Why haven't you called?'; 'Let me know when you've told him.'; 'Please, Hannah; you promised.'

At 8.56 a.m. she sent me a two-word text: *It's over.*

Monday

10.55 am

I'd not heard from Hannah since her two-word text. Meeting face to face again was bound to be awkward, so I was kind of relieved to have avoided her until first break. The best-case scenario was a touching reconciliation scene where we hugged tearfully and she thanked me for being a good friend. Only I wasn't sure that Hannah would see it that way.

And what about Mr Moore? It was double Drama before lunch. How could I just sit there as if nothing had happened? I hated him for what he'd done. And it hurt like hell that someone I'd practically idolised could let me down like that.

Normally I'd have been looking out for her. 'Accidentally' bumping into Hannah was a favourite pastime of mine. This time, I kept my head down, scuttling across the courtyard in the hopes of delaying a difficult encounter for a few minutes longer. But it wasn't to be.

'Hello, Beth. Could I have a quick word please?' She looked like she'd been crying again. And she'd done something different to her hair.

'What is it?'

Miss Hoolyhan reached for her Statue-of-Liberty earrings. 'Don't worry, you're not in trouble or anything. Mr Edmonds wants to see you, that's all.'

The last time I'd had any contact with our 'glorious' headteacher was when my French essay ('*La Vie Scholaire*') won a Special Achievement Award in Year Nine. 'What does he want?'

'I'm . . . not sure,' said Miss Hoolyhan, whose lying skills obviously needed some serious attention. 'But if you pop across to main reception and wait outside his office, someone will be out to get you.'

'Shouldn't I leave it until after registration?'

'*No*,' said Miss Hoolyhan. 'I think you'd better go now. And Beth?'

'Yes.'

Short hair suited her. She made a much better pixie than a witch. 'I just wanted you to know that . . .' Her mouth fell open, but the words seemed to stick in her throat. 'Never mind; doesn't matter.'

It didn't feel like a good omen when the woman in reception recognised me instantly. 'Ah Beth,' she said, grabbing her phone and tapping in an extension number. 'Take a seat. I'll let Mr Edmonds know you're here.'

I really didn't need this, and today of all days. A few years back, I'd have been terrified that something had happened to Dad. After Mum died, I developed a kind of obsession about losing him in a plane crash. But like he said, the odds of that were ten million to one – besides he wasn't even flying until the end of the week. My work was fine too. So what was it all about?

Main reception felt like the health centre waiting room, except instead of doctor photos, there was a scary image of Mr Edmonds surrounded by his prefects, like a modern-day Fagin.

The bald bloke opposite, sipping coffee and chain-eating chocolate digestives, was sweating like a sumo wrestler. I recognised him from the posters in the Learning Resources Centre. He was another one of those writers who turned up at school far too frequently, bored you silly with a creative writing workshop ('Show don't tell – blah blah blah') and then tried to flog you their terrible books. No wonder he looked nervous.

'It's like Clapham Junction in there,' he said, nodding at Mr Edmonds's office. 'What do you think's going on?'

'I don't know,' I said, suddenly remembering what Mum once told me about writers: *They'll steal your life-story and try to pass it off as their imagination.* 'I expect it's something to do with the OFSTED inspection.'

'Oh well,' he said, polishing off the last chocolate digestive. 'Worse things have happened at sea.'

But I was struggling to imagine any of them when the door opened and out popped Mr Catchpole. 'Ah Beth, you're here, good, just wait there a moment, I need to . . .' He turned to the balding writer. 'I'm terribly sorry, I'm afraid we're going to have to postpone this morning's visit. We'll make sure you get your fee, of course.'

'I don't actually get a . . . What's the trouble anyway?' said the writer, hopefully.

Mr Catchpole handed him his brimming box of paperbacks. 'Oh, just some . . . time-tabling issues. Here, why don't I help you with the door?'

The moment he'd gone, Mr Catchpole dashed across to the Head's office and knocked three times. 'You'd better go in, Beth. I need to make a couple of phone calls.'

Mr Edmonds didn't look at all like his photo. His teeth stayed well hidden and the expansive hand gestures he'd used so unsparingly in his promo-film for prospective parents (*Reach for the A-Stars*) were replaced by tightly folded arms.

'Good morning, Beth.'

'Good . . . morning.'

Seated opposite him was a man in a blue suit and a woman with a shopping bag bulging with empty cereal boxes who turned directly she heard my voice.

'Where the hell is she?'

It was Hannah's mum. But she was almost unrecognisable as the guardian angel who'd sent me home with a week's supply of Viennese Fingers.

'Calm down, love,' said the man in the blue suit. 'Give her a chance.'

'No I will not calm down. Not until she tells me where she is.'

Mr Edmonds loosened his tie and coughed. 'This is Mr and Mrs Poole, Beth; Hannah Taylor's parents.'

'She knows who I am,' said Steph Poole. 'Just ask her where Hannah is!'

'Come on, love,' said the man who must have been Alan, and didn't seem half as bad as his stepdaughter made out. 'This isn't helping.'

Steph Poole nodded apologetically. 'I know, I'm sorry, I didn't mean to shout at you, Beth. It's just . . .'

Alan draped his arm around her. 'Don't worry, Stephie. It's going to be all right.'

Mr Edmonds smiled like a healthcare professional about to break bad news. 'Hannah isn't in school this morning.'

'Oh . . . right,' I said, half relieved that I wouldn't be bumping into her.

Mr Edmonds reached for his unusually bulbous earlobe. 'Apparently Hannah was with you last night.'

'Who told you that?' I said.

'She did,' said her mum. 'She said she was sleeping over at your house so you could rehearse the play.'

'Well it's not true,' I said.

'She's lying,' said Steph Poole. 'Ask her about the text.'

'What text?' I said.

Alan waved a mobile phone at me. 'She sent Steph a message at five o'clock this morning: *Sorry Mum it's the only way.*'

'I honestly don't know anything about it,' I said. 'I haven't seen Hannah since Saturday morning.'

'Yes, and she'd been in a foul mood ever since.' Steph Poole let out a howl of pain. 'Oh dear God, what has she done?'

'Now I want you to think very carefully, Beth,' said Mr Edmonds, eyeing me deliberately, like he was looking for the 'correct' answer. 'Have you any idea why Hannah might not be in school this morning?'

I reached instinctively for the nearest lie. 'Perhaps you should try her dad in Milton Keynes.'

'We already did,' said Alan. 'No luck I'm afraid.'

I couldn't tell them what I was really thinking. Steph Poole was in a bad enough state already. But I was replaying what Hannah said at the first rehearsal: *If you really loved someone, you couldn't live without them.* No matter how hard I tried to put the idea out of my head, it kept creeping back. I'd seen the way she looked when I told her to finish with him. Who knows what she was capable of? Maybe I shouldn't have pushed her into it. Maybe I should have gone straight to Mr Edmonds. Maybe Hannah wasn't as strong as I thought. If anything had happened to her, I'd never forgive myself.

Her mum was obviously thinking the same thing. 'Why didn't I talk to her? I knew something was wrong. You know what she's like, Al. Her hormones are all over the place. A girl like that on her own; it just doesn't bear . . . Supposing she goes and does something silly?'

Mr Edmonds seemed to have other ideas. 'Let's not jump to any conclusions,' he said, twisting uncomfortably in his ergonomic office chair. 'I'm sure she'll turn up safe and well. As I say, the police have been informed and Mr Catchpole is exploring other . . . possibilities.'

'Like what?' said Hannah's mother. 'Is there something you're not telling me?'

'You'd better get off to your next lesson, Beth,' said Mr Edmonds. 'And Beth, if you do think of something, you will let me know?'

I was too shell-shocked to do anything but nod obediently and stumble to the door. And that's how I stayed until the end of the morning, when I walked into double Drama and sniffed the air.

Her perfume preceded her like poison gas. There was a gasp of horror as Miss Carver, who looked about as happy to see us as we were to see her, walked to the end of Brighton Pier and threw herself off.

'Right, this morning I'm going have a look at your improvised performance pieces.'

'Where's Mr Moore?' said Duncan Fox.

'Mr Moore is . . . unwell,' said Miss Carver, who

looked pretty exhausted herself. 'I'm really not sure when he'll be back.'

'What about *Romeo and Juliet*?'

'*Who?*' said Miss Carver. 'Oh right, yes. We'll have to see about that, I suppose.'

Don't ask me why, I just knew. There were a hundred and one different explanations for both of them not turning up to school on the same day but I was so certain, that, just for a millisecond, all I felt was a sense of relief.

Hannah wasn't alone at all. She was with Mr Moore.

But relief soon soured into guilt. I was the only person in the whole school who'd known what they were up to. Why hadn't I said something? And why was I keeping quiet now? It was pretty messed up I know, but I hadn't forgotten my promise to Hannah. Even after everything she'd done, I still couldn't bring myself to break it.

But that wasn't the only thing. I had this terrible feeling that if I did tell someone, they'd say it was all my fault. So I kept my mouth shut, hoping that I wouldn't have to. Maybe Mr Moore had texted Sarah and Archie. Surely it couldn't be long before someone else put two and two together.

2.20 pm

I had a fair idea why Mr Edmonds had summoned the whole of Years Ten and Eleven to the Main Hall after registration, but the other theories on offer were the usual St Thomas's blend of satire and paranoia:

153

'I reckon that Shezza girl's pregnant. Have you seen the size of her?'

'It's probably about that kid with cancer. You're not supposed to come into school if you've got a . . .' They all faked a massive sneeze.

'He's not going to cancel the prom, is he? Remember what Catchpole said about three strikes and you're out?'

'Maybe they've found the phantom YouTuber.'

'So long as no one's died again; remember that, it was a right pain?'

Mr Catchpole certainly looked like he was in mourning. He stood ashen-faced at the side of the stage, directing operations like a power-crazed undertaker. 'Hurry along please. Take your seats as quickly as possible. And keep the noise down. It's important that you listen carefully to what Mr Edmonds has to say.'

'You're not leaving are you, sir?' enquired a 'well-wisher'.

'No, Liam, I'm not leaving.'

'Shame.'

Mr Catchpole ignored the raucous laughter. He didn't even reward Liam Corcoran with a week in detention. It was serious all right. His only concern was Miss Hoolyhan and her straggle of latecomers. 'Hurry along, please. And make sure you all have your phones switched off. I will not ask again.'

A few months ago, Mr Catchpole's 'mindless vandalism' lecture turned up on YouTube; the culprit had yet to be found.

Miss Hoolyhan was shrouded in a white silk scarf, a stark contrast to the reds of her eyes. 'Settle down everyone. Let's have a bit of hush.'

'What's going on, miss?' said Duncan Fox.

'I don't know, Duncan. I'm not a mind-reader. I wish I was.'

Mr Edmonds walked purposefully down the centre aisle. Once on stage however, he froze, tapping the radio mic with his index finger and glancing anxiously at Mr Catchpole. He normally ad-libbed for what seemed like hours, but this time he was obviously reading from notes. 'Good afternoon.'

AJ and Candice didn't seem to have noticed their 'friend' Hannah's unauthorised absence. They were more worried about the windswept state of their harassed headteacher. 'Doesn't his hair look gross?'

'Sometimes in the life of a school,' continued Mr Edmonds, 'unforeseen circumstances can present us with new and potentially complex challenges.'

'Yeah, like split ends,' whispered AJ.

'That's why this afternoon, I'm asking for your cooperation. As senior members of the school cohort, I know I can count on you to treat what I am about to say with suitable maturity.'

'Told you someone was pregnant,' whispered Candice Barrett.

'Don't be an idiot,' said AJ. 'Why would Edmonds announce it in assembly? Chelsey whatsherface put her baby-scan photos on Facebook.'

Mr Edmonds paused for a moment to study his notes. 'At some point in the next forty-eight hours, you will probably be hearing "allegations" about a St Thomas's pupil and a member of staff.'

The shocked silence was soon broken by a chorus of belly laughs and giggles.

'Oh my God,' said AJ. 'That is well funny.'

'What kind of allegations?' said Candice Barrett.

'Quiet, please!' said Mr Catchpole. 'This is important.'

'I can neither confirm nor deny anything at this stage,' said Mr Edmonds. 'However, I know I can trust you not to jump to any premature conclusions. Of course, if you do have any concrete information, I would urge you to come forward. Here at St Thomas's we are a close-knit community.'

'Bit too close if you ask me,' said AJ.

'Unfortunately, it's quite possible that there may be some media speculation. So I would ask you, respectfully, not to add to this.'

'Who do you reckon it is?' whispered Candice Barrett.

Mr Edmonds tugged at his earlobe. 'As you all know, we have a robust child-protection policy, which I shall be outlining very shortly on ParentMail. Thank you. That's all.'

He was halfway across the stage before the main hall erupted in a frenzy of wild speculation.

'It's probably Mr Willcock and that kid in the football team.'

'Or the supply teacher with the wonky eye.'

'What about Mr Peel. He's always on about that shitty band of his.'

'Who says it's a bloke anyway?'

Grunt was waiting for me in the corridor. I tried to keep walking, but he wouldn't let me pass. 'It's Hannah Taylor, isn't it? It's Hannah Taylor and Mr Moore. I'm right, aren't I, Beth?'

'How should I know?'

It couldn't stay a secret much longer anyway. They'd all find out soon enough.

6.30 pm

That night it made the local News. Dad was unloading a tea-chest full of junk that he'd lugged up from the shed when Hannah's school photo flashed onto the telly.

'The search has begun for missing schoolgirl, Hannah Taylor, who disappeared from her home at the weekend.'

'Hang on a minute, that's your friend, isn't it?' said Dad, laying out a parade of scantily-clad Barbies on the coffee table.

'Yeah.'

Hannah's head gave way to some random footage of that oily MP opening the new science block.

'The fifteen-year-old, who is a pupil at St Thomas's Community College, is believed to have been accompanied by a member of staff.'

'Bloody hell,' said Dad. 'What kind of a school is that Edmonds bloke running?'

I don't know where they'd found the photo of Mr Moore, but he looked like the Child Catcher from *Chitty Chitty Bang Bang*.

'Twenty-seven-year-old Steven Moore is a temporary Drama teacher and the father of twins. A spokesman from the school declined to comment. Police have asked members of the public to—'

'Hey, I was watching that,' said Dad.

'Sorry, I just didn't want to . . .'

Dad slid across the sofa towards me. 'That's the new Drama teacher, isn't it? Isn't he the one who's doing the play?'

'Yes.'

'And you had no idea that this was going on?'

Lying still felt like the safest option. 'No, of course not.'

'That's often the way,' said Dad. 'People like that can be very devious. They want stringing up if you ask me.'

All I could think about was Hannah. I still wasn't sure if I'd let her down.

'Now listen Beth, have you any idea where they might be?'

At last, I could answer truthfully. 'No, haven't a clue.'

'And had she ever talked about running away?'

'No, never,' I said. 'Why all the questions, anyway?'

'Because you were such good friends,' said Dad. 'I'm sure the police will want to talk to you.'

Horrible as that sounded, I'd still felt a quiver of guilty pleasure when he called us good friends. 'What for?'

'They'll be trying to track them down,' said Dad. 'You might just know something that could help.'

I hadn't a clue where they might be. London perhaps, or a remote Scottish island like the one in Grunt's game? But wherever they were, I couldn't help imagining how it would be for them – life on the run, seeing yourself on the News, constantly looking over your shoulder. And you know the craziest thing of all? Underneath the anger, my fear for Hannah's safety and the enormity of the black hole that she'd dug for herself, a small part of me was just the tiniest bit jealous.

'What on earth was the silly girl thinking of?' said Dad, reaching into the tea-chest and pulling out a Polly Pocket ambulance. 'Thank goodness you've got more sense.'

10.30 pm

I was staring at the shadows on the ceiling when my phone started jiggling on the bedside table. It wasn't a number I recognised. Dad, Grunt and Hannah were the only names in my contacts list. It was a bit late to be selling insurance.

'Who is this please?'

'Hello, stranger!'

I couldn't get over how excited she sounded. 'Where are you?'

And now she was laughing at me. 'Do you think I'm stupid or something?'

'Yes, I do actually, Hannah. What are you playing at?

I told you I wouldn't say anything. All you had to do was finish with him.'

'What else could we do? We just want to be together. Why does no one understand that?'

I felt sick. 'Come off it, Hannah, this isn't *Romeo and Juliet*.'

'Well let's hope not, because we both know how that one turned out.'

She still didn't get it. 'Where is he anyway? Where's Mr Moore?'

'Steve's in the shower,' she said, a knowing smile in her voice. 'He'd flip out if he knew I was calling you.'

'Where are you, in a hotel or something?'

'Look, I can't say.'

'Are you . . . frightened of him, Hannah?'

'Don't be silly. He's just a bit paranoid about covering our tracks. We dumped our mobiles in the river. But I managed to jot down your number first. He doesn't know I've got a new one. It is so cool, babe. Just like yours.'

'Where did you get it?'

'Found it on the train, didn't I? If you leave one of these babies in the toilet you deserve to have it nicked.'

'Train, what train? And which river are you talking about – not the Thames? Where are you? You have to tell me!'

'Yeah, right.'

'Please, look, you have to come home – this is insane.'

'Stop it,' said Hannah. 'I wish I hadn't phoned you now.'

'Yeah, why *did* you phone me?'

For the first time, I detected a note of uncertainty. 'Because we're friends, aren't we? I thought you'd want to know that I was okay.'

I'd been thinking about that too. 'Friends – is that what we are, Hannah? Funny, because *I* think you were just using me. You told your mum you were staying at mine, didn't you? And I bet that wasn't the only time.'

The other end went dead.

'Hannah, Hannah – are you still there?'

'Yeah, I wanted to say sorry about that too. I shouldn't have used you as an excuse. But we *are* friends Beth, you know that, don't you? You're the only one I can trust.'

Her tears were obviously catching. 'And are you really okay?'

'Think so,' she said. 'At least I will be if everyone leaves us alone.'

'Listen, Hannah, you've got to call your mum. I saw her in school this morning. That text you sent her really freaked her out.'

'I can't face it. I'll send her an e-mail when we get settled somewhere.'

'Let me tell her for you then. Or I could give her your number if you like.'

There was a real edge to her voice. 'No, don't. And you mustn't tell anyone you've spoken to me.'

'Why not, I —'

'I mean it, Beth. Keep your bloody mouth shut.'

'I'm not sure I can —'

161

'Look, either you promise not to say anything, or I dump this phone right now and you'll never hear from me again.'

'Well I —'

'Please Beth, I just don't think I can do this on my own.'

I didn't have much choice. If she thought the whole world was against her, who knows what she might do. At least this way I could be sure she was still okay. She trusted me. Maybe if we stayed in contact, I could persuade her to come home. 'Yeah, all right then. But you've got to promise *me* something too.'

'What?'

'I need to speak to you every day. I'll call you, okay?'

'No you can't. If I leave my phone on the whole time the battery will run out. And anyway, he mustn't know I've got one. I'll contact you when I can.'

What else could I do? 'Well don't let me down again, okay?'

Her sigh of relief whooshed down the receiver. 'I really do love him you know, Beth. And he loves me too. You do believe me, don't you?'

I'd keep her secret for the moment, but I wasn't going to lie to her. 'I think you should come home, Hannah. You can't —'

'Gotta go,' she whispered. 'Talk to you later, babe. Wish me —'

Tuesday

1.35 pm

I'd spent half the morning lying, first to Mr Catchpole
and then the plain clothes police officer who'd set herself
up in the temporary classrooms and wanted to speak
to all Hannah's friends. The school nurse chaperoned
twitchily in the background, while DS Vanessa Whitfield
(that was the name on her lanyard) quizzed me about
Mr Moore and Hannah.

'What was your opinion of Mr Moore as a teacher?'
('He was pretty good, I suppose.')

'How would you describe his relationship with
Hannah Taylor?' ('Well, just normal, I guess.')

'What did Hannah say about Mr Moore?' ('Not a lot
really.')

'Tell me about Hannah's state of mind the last time you

saw her.' ('She was always a bit moody before she came on. But I know she was looking forward to the play.')

'Do you have any idea where Hannah might be?' (And finally, a truthful 'No.')

Ms Whitfield was all smiles and friendliness. But it was a slick, professional kind of friendliness, like an MP or a children's television presenter. I knew very well she was digging for dirt on Mr Moore. And I would love to have dished her some. But I'd made a promise to Hannah, and I wasn't about to break it yet. So I stuck to short answers, knowing my lying skills would never extend to full paragraphs.

It was the last question that threw me. Miss Hoolyhan must have told her about the poetry gig in Brighton, because she wanted to know why I'd been there, and whether Mr Moore's offer of a lift had seemed 'unusual at all'. It's lucky she didn't have a lie detector, because the crap I came out with about the 'visceral power' of performance poetry was plain embarrassing. But it was a lot less embarrassing than what I didn't tell her: about my crush on Mr Moore, or how elated I'd felt when he offered to drive us home.

It was a relief to get out of there. That is, until I realised it was lunchtime and the subject of a certain Drama teacher and his star pupil was trending all over the school.

Down in the courtyard, they were trading the latest 'Mooretaylor' jokes.

'What's Hannah's favourite whisky?' ('Teachers.')

'Why did Mr Moore cross the road?' ('To get to the Taylor on the other side.')

'What's the difference between Hannah Taylor and a rubbish actress?' ('Hannah's had more Drama teachers.')

Even the Year Sevens behind the recycling bins were debating what a hot girl like Hannah Taylor was doing with an old guy like Mr Moore.

It wasn't much better in the canteen. Pete Hughes was trialling a new catchphrase, which he repeated to everyone he thought had missed it the first time. 'Please sir, I want some Moore.'

It was obvious what AJ and the rest of them were laughing at. But they soon stopped when I joined the queue.

'Look who it is,' said Candice Barrett. 'It's the chief bridesmaid.'

'So where's Hannah then?' said AJ. 'Where's your little bestie and pervy Steve?'

'Don't know what you're talking about,' I said.

'Come off it,' said Candice Barrett. 'I bet it was your idea in the first place.'

'Yes,' said AJ. 'No offence or anything, but she was never a slut until she started hanging out with you.'

Candice Barrett glowered with mock solemnity. 'Yeah, that can happen sometimes – good girls going bad. All they have to do is fall in with the wrong person.'

'Just leave her alone,' said a voice from the back of the queue. 'Beth's got nothing to do with it.'

'Oh look,' says AJ. 'It's the poster-boy for fat camp.'

Grunt blushed, like he always did when a girl spoke to him. 'You ought to be ashamed of yourselves. I thought Hannah Taylor was supposed to be your friend.'

'You must be joking,' said Candice Barrett. 'After what she's done?'

AJ nodded her agreement. 'Never did like her much anyway. We were at primary school together, you know. That girl's so up herself she's practically invisible.'

'Nice one,' said Candice Barrett, exchanging a bitchy high-five. 'And she was even worse after she started that play. Look at the way she treated poor Duncan.'

'And now we know why, the little skank,' added AJ.

'Don't call her that,' I said.

'So*rree*,' said AJ. 'If she was so worried about her reputation, she should have kept her hands off him.'

'Yeah, and I'll tell you something else,' said Candice Barrett. 'She was a crap actress too.'

Support came from a rather unexpected source. Dave Denyer was sitting alone, a half-eaten pannini in front of him and a look of abject misery on his face. 'You don't know anything. Hannah's Juliet was amazing. And you know why? Because she never faked it. Okay, so she's messed up big time. But at least she's not a two-faced bitch like you.'

'Yeah, whatever,' said AJ, grabbing a fruit slushie and making a beeline for her favourite table.

'Hey Beth,' called Dave Denyer.

'Yes?' I said, half expecting him to have a go at me too.

'Do you think she might come back to do the play?'

'Probably not, Dave. And even if she did, I doubt they'd let her do it.'

'Yeah, that's what I thought,' said Dave Denyer, so dejected that he barely acknowledged the Year Seven with a death wish, who accidentally bumped into him on his way to the door.

I wasn't hungry any more. But I selected a tuna pannini, pressed my finger against the sensor, and stared despairingly into the gossip-guzzling canteen.

'You okay?' said Grunt.

'Why shouldn't I be?'

Grunt licked his lips. 'You can sit with me if you like.'

'Thanks.'

I followed him to the table we'd shared every lunchtime until Hannah came on the scene. *His* appetite was as healthy as ever. 'Where do you think they are?'

'I don't know.'

Grunt shovelled spicy sausage pasta, somehow managing to talk at the same time. 'Did you have any idea what was going on?'

I was *that* close to telling him. 'No.'

'It's all over Twitter. You should see what they're saying about her.'

'What about him?' I said. 'He's the one they should be talking about.'

'Yeah, him too,' said Grunt. 'But there are loads more photos of Hannah.'

'Typical.'

'You'd better have a look at this,' he said, handing me his phone. 'I reckon it was AJ and that lot.'

The 'Steve and Hannah Condolence Page' already had 307 Likes. They'd photo-shopped a wedding picture. Mr Moore's suit was covered in arrows like a cartoon convict and beneath her white veil Hannah was wearing full school uniform. The slogan read: *Hey girl, did you know that you don't have to show the Drama teacher all your best parts?*

And underneath, her so-called 'cool' friends were queuing up to slag her off. Some of the comments were so vile I threw Grunt's phone back at him like an unexploded bomb. 'That is so horrible. Do you reckon Hannah will see all this?'

'Of course she will,' said Grunt. 'She's not going to stop checking her Facebook page just because she's run off with Mr Moore.'

He was right. You couldn't run away properly any more. It didn't matter where you went; whatever you were running from was never more than two clicks away. 'I just wish she'd . . .'

'I warned you about her, didn't I?' said Grunt.

'Eh?'

'I told you Hannah Taylor was bad news.'

'Hang on a minute. Are you saying this is Hannah's fault?'

'Well it takes two to . . . no course not.'

I wanted to smear sausage pasta all over his smug

little face. But he'd made a pretty good job of it himself. 'You're unbelievable. She's fifteen. He's a teacher. Don't you get it?'

'Yes but —'

'You're as bad as the rest of them.'

'Sit down. Let's just —'

But it was much too late for that. 'Don't talk to me, okay? Don't *ever* talk to me. In fact, don't even look at me. I never want to see you again.'

Red-faced with fury, I swatted Year Sevens as I scrambled for the door.

And somewhere in the distance, AJ and Candice Barrett squealed with delight.

6.04 pm

'You'd better come in here, Beth,' called Dad.

'In a minute; the sauce isn't ready yet.'

'Hurry up or you'll miss it.'

He sounded pretty insistent, so I chucked a handful of tarragon in the saucepan and turned down the hob.

It wasn't like Dad to be glued to the telly. Not unless it was a documentary about Victorian sewers or the Vietnam War. But I soon saw why.

She might have been wearing a smart business suit, but Hannah's mum looked a mess. She took a sip of water, glanced sideways at Alan and then turned towards the flashing barrage of cameras, her high definition tears trickling down the screen like it was raining inside the telly.

169

'. . . so please darling, just tell us where you are. We have to know that you're safe. And don't worry, you're not in any trouble. I'm here for you, Hannah. All I want is to . . . All I want is to . . . sorry . . .' The cameras clicked even louder as she tried to compose herself. 'Nathan's missing you like crazy. I can't even get him to school. He says he wants to stay home and wait for you. Please, Hannah. I know you're probably confused and . . . everything. But please, darling . . . *please*. We just want you back.'

A uniformed police officer brought the press conference to a close, urging the public to stay vigilant and advising 'Steve' to do the best thing for Hannah and bring her home.

'Poor woman,' said Dad, who'd been sorting through a pile of ancient biscuit tins he'd found in the old coal-bunker. 'Did you know her at all?'

'Yeah, a little bit,' I said. 'Steph's actually really nice.'

'God knows what must be going through her head.' A transfusion of guilt coursed through my veins.

Mr Edmonds appeared on the TV. His body language – standing outside the Business Enterprise Centre, blinking too often, arms tightly folded across his chest – had a touch of guilt about it too. 'Of course our thoughts at this time go out to Hannah's family. But I want to make it very clear that this was an isolated incident. Our child-protection policy is fully in line with government recommendations and subject to . . . constant review.'

Next there were a few seconds of Mr Moore's

performance poetry with the swear words bleeped, and a couple more of the '£250,000 house he shared with his partner Sarah and their son Albert'.

But, as always over the coming days, they finished with a photo of Hannah, this time in a sleeveless yellow top that must have been taken during that really hot afternoon on the war graves trip.

I wondered if Hannah was watching somewhere. How would it feel to see your mum in so much pain? I knew the answer to that one. But I couldn't begin to imagine having my whole life on display like that. I just hoped that Hannah could handle it. If things started going wrong for her, I had a nasty feeling she might do something silly.

10.43 pm

After I'd calmed down a bit, I took the iPad upstairs and forced myself to read what people were saying about them. A simple search for *Steve and Hannah* brought up thirty million results in 0.14 seconds.

There was a real desperation to find something to blame: the school, the parents, the decline of organised religion, mobile phones, advertising, social media, the benefits culture, that 1970s DJ.

Some even saw the whole thing as *Much Ado About Nothing* or a twenty-first century version of *Romeo and Juliet*.

And the rest were so repulsive I could hardly bear to look: half about what they'd like to do to Mr Moore;

the other half about what they wanted to do to Hannah.

But most shocking of all was the red-lettered headline when I returned to my homepage.

Breaking News:
Runaway Schoolgirl and Drama Teacher
Sighted at Victoria Station

Wednesday

10.35 am

'Hey sir, will Hannah Taylor still get fined for going on holiday in term time if she's with a teacher?'

Mr Catchpole already had the weight of the world on his shoulders. 'Thank you Candice, that's enough.'

We'd all seen it on *Breakfast Time* – the CCTV footage of Hannah and Mr Moore at Victoria Station, and the interview with the guy from WH Smith who'd sold them two Mars bars and a copy of *Vogue* and was pretty sure he recognised Hannah from the pictures at the press conference.

The acting director of Student Welfare looked like he hadn't slept for a week. He'd already warned us that the subject was strictly off limits, but that didn't stop his Year Eleven PSHE class bombarding him with their thoughts on the matter.

'Do you think if she'd had decent PSHE lessons, Hannah would have learned to make better choices?'

'Yeah. We've done Stranger Danger, but we've never done Teacher Alert.'

AJ had her hand up. 'If Hannah and Mr Moore get married, sir, will you go to the wedding?'

Mr Catchpole was not amused. 'Look, this isn't funny. A child is missing. I know you people mask your anxieties behind an impenetrable wall of sarcasm, but what's happened is deeply troubling for us all. If you have any concerns you should talk privately to a member of staff.'

'I don't think so,' said AJ. 'What if they hit on me?'

'For pity's sake,' said Mr Catchpole, slamming his hand down on the table. 'I've been teaching at this school for over seven years. And I cannot recall a single incident that has . . .'

I missed the next bit, because right in the middle of the acting director of Student Welfare's public meltdown, I felt my phone vibrate. Someone was texting me. And it had to be Hannah. But I didn't dare sneak it out of my pocket. Even on the verge of a nervous breakdown, Mr Catchpole could sniff a mobile a mile off. I couldn't risk it being confiscated. It was our only means of communication.

As soon as the lesson was over, I raced down to the bottom of the field. The tree they'd planted in memory of the boy who died in the car crash still wasn't tall enough

174

to shelter me from the teeming rain, so I crouched behind it, careful that not even the masochists from the jogging club could spot me on their way past.

Hannah's message was short and bitter. Not to mention exactly the sort of thing I'd been dreading: *Saw what they're saying about us. Why can't they leave us alone?*

I tried to call her, but went straight through to voicemail.

'*Hannah* . . . listen, Hannah, you need to call me. I just want to know that you're all right. And I need to hear your voice. You promised, remember? So just . . . call me, okay?'

3.27 pm
We'd been warned about a million times not to speak to them, but that wasn't stopping AJ giving the performance of her life in front of one of the numerous film crews that had started turning up after school.

'I couldn't believe it,' she said. 'Hannah was, like, my best friend, yeah? We'd known each other since primary school.'

I stood in the background with the other St Thomas's thrill-seekers. Not, like most of them, because I was desperate to get my face on television, but because there was an outside chance that the woman behind the camera might just have some new information about Hannah. I was so worried about her. Every couple of hours I'd leave a new message begging her to contact me, but she still hadn't called. Where the hell were they?

My imagination was working overtime.

'I just wish she'd told me,' said AJ, her fake tears lapping at her surprisingly pristine mascara. 'If anyone could have stopped her, it was me.'

The woman behind the camera was obviously relishing every moment of it. 'And is there anything you'd like to say to Hannah?'

'Please come back, babe. We all miss you. We don't care what you've done. We just want you back.'

I felt like throwing up. Hannah was my friend, not AJ's – at least, not any more. It should have been me up there, not her. And part of me wanted to tell them everything. But I'd promised Hannah to keep quiet, so I grabbed a metaphorical sick bag and willed the little bitch to stop.

Luckily Mr Catchpole was on the case. He charged towards the school gates like an arthritic bull and pulled up panting in front of the camera. 'I thought I warned you about this.'

The woman behind the camera smiled sweetly. 'And as I said before, Colin, this is a public interest story. The British people have a right to know.'

'Anisette is a minor,' said Mr Catchpole. 'Has her parent or guardian signed a consent form?'

'It's all right, sir,' said AJ. 'My mum'll be fine about it.'

And that's when my phone went – with the camera still running and surrounded by half of Year Eleven. I knew immediately it was Hannah. But there was no way I could answer it, especially with so many journalists sniffing about. All I could do was tap ignore, and sneak it back into my pocket.

Meanwhile, Mr Catchpole was turning crimson. 'This is quite clearly a safeguarding issue. If you continue with the interview, I'm afraid I'll have to call the police.'

'I'm sorry, Colin,' said the woman behind the camera. 'Perhaps you'd like to speak to us yourself. Maybe you could quash some of the rumours about your senior management team.'

'Mr Edmonds made a statement yesterday. We won't be commenting further until the issue is resolved.' His voice softened as he turned to AJ. 'Now go home, Anisette. I don't know what you were hoping to achieve here, but you're certainly not helping Hannah.'

Hannah needed all the help she could get. I didn't dare listen to her message until I was safely back in my bedroom. And every time I played it, she sounded a little bit worse:

'Where are you? Why aren't you picking up? Don't do this to me Beth. It's a bloody waste of battery for a start. And if I don't talk to someone soon I'll go . . .'

Her voice fell to a teary whisper. 'Steve says we've got to move on again. He's left me here while he goes to buy train tickets. Some bloke gave him a funny look and now he's wetting himself. He's so moody lately. One minute he's all like, *Everything's going to be fine*, and the next thing you know he's telling me we might as well give up running because they're bound to catch us in the end. I don't think I could stand that. If I can't be with him, I think I'd rather . . .'

The teary whisper got even quieter. 'Look, if anything happens to me, tell Mum I . . .'

But she couldn't finish her sentence.

Thursday

10.08 pm

In a strange way, it brought us closer. Every few hours, we'd assemble in the lounge for the latest News bulletin. Dad obviously saw how worried I was. In fact, I only narrowly persuaded him not to pull out of his weekend flight to Los Angeles.

By Thursday evening they were the second story on the Ten O'Clock News. It seemed like half the world was looking for them. But they hadn't made much progress. Apart from a possible sighting in Edinburgh and an internet theory that Mr Moore had contacts in South America, the trail seemed to have gone dead.

It might have looked like fun in the movies, but I was pretty sure that real life on the run would be a nightmare. And I certainly wasn't jealous any more. Poor Hannah;

I couldn't begin to imagine how she felt.

But I didn't have to, because after an ex-teacher had discussed the difficulty of pupil/teacher relationships in the age of Facebook, there was an interview with a child psychiatrist from our local CAMHS office.

I'd never heard of Dr Kim Tennant, although apparently she'd treated plenty of kids from St Thomas's in her time. 'I don't know Hannah, of course,' she said. 'But I would imagine she's very frightened right now. Perhaps to begin with she was caught up in the adventure of it all, but I'm quite sure she never imagined the situation developing in this way.'

'And how about her teacher, Steven Moore?'

'That's more difficult to say. It's possible he feels exactly the same. One thing's for certain – Hannah will become increasingly reliant on him. Whatever she thinks she feels for this man, it's bound to be intensified.'

'Some people are calling this a love story. Can a relationship between a schoolgirl of fifteen and a twenty-seven-year-old adult ever be the real thing?'

'No . . . no, of course not,' said Dr Tennant, looking like she wanted to disappear into her flowery blouse, 'especially if the older person is an authority figure. Hannah might well believe that her feelings are genuine, but it could never be an equal partnership.'

'Do you think Hannah is in any danger?'

'It depends what you mean by danger. There'll almost certainly be some long-term emotional damage – trust issues perhaps. And Hannah's very vulnerable right now.

180

It's possible she could overreact.'

'What do you mean by that?'

'Well . . . if Hannah feels under pressure, she might behave irrationally.'

'So what would you say to her if she was with you right now?'

Dr Tennant eyeballed the camera like a TV hypnotist. 'Come home, Hannah. Your family loves you. It may seem like an impossible situation, but all this can be sorted, it's not too late. And please don't be coerced into something you might later regret. You see, it's —'

'I think I'll go up,' I said, unable to stand much more of it.

'Are you sure?' said Dad. 'Look, if there's something you want to talk about, I—'

'No, no, it's okay, Dad. I'll see you in the morning.'

'Righty-ho then,' he said, not quite managing to hide his relief. 'I'm just going to have a quick look in the garage and then I think I'll get an early night too.'

That psychiatrist had scared the life out of me. If she thought Hannah was in danger before, how would she feel if she heard her message? I must have played it at least fifty times. At first, I tried to identify any background noises that might give me a clue as to where they were headed. But I soon forgot about the high-pitched whistle and the crackly murmur that might just have been a station announcer. All I could hear was Hannah's pain.

So before I climbed into bed for another eight hours of wide-eyed anxiety, I left her yet another message: 'Look, I'm really sorry I couldn't call back before, but please, please, please, please, please, please, please, please, *please* call me back, Hannah. I'm so worried about you.'

Friday

7.15 pm

The St Thomas's rumours were more outrageous every time I checked Facebook. Some had them tying the knot in a gypsy ceremony in Verona, others drugs-running in Thailand, whilst Candice and AJ insisted that Mr Moore had already dumped Hannah for a younger model. Meanwhile, I was back in my bedroom, shouting at Hannah's voicemail:

'We had an agreement, Hannah. Look, you don't have to speak to me if you don't want to. Leave another message or something. I need to be sure that nothing bad has happened. Just call me, okay? Or I'll have to tell them everything I know. So don't be so bloody selfish you silly stupid —'

Dad knocked on the door. 'Are you all right in there?'

'Yes, Dad. Don't come in, I —'

Too late, he was already standing in the doorway. 'Who were you talking to?'

'Just George,' I said, tossing my phone onto the bed and trying to look innocent.

'I thought you two had fallen out.'

'Yeah, we had. But we kind of made up.'

'Didn't sound like it,' said Dad, whose strange smile was unnerving me.

'Did you want something, Dad?'

'Yes I do as it happens. Why don't you come downstairs for a bit? I've got a little surprise for you.'

He was off to LA in the morning – the six o'clock flight, so I wouldn't even see him. It was probably another guilt offering. 'Couldn't it wait until later, when I come down for the News?'

If anything, his strange smile was widening. 'I don't think it could actually. You see, I've found what I was looking for. And I think you're going to like it.'

He'd been searching the house from top to bottom. At least there'd be no more Kilimanjaros of junk. 'Okay, fine. What is it anyway?'

'Come and see for yourself.'

I followed obediently to the lounge.

'Take a seat,' said Dad. 'I won't be a sec.'

It was attached to the side of the telly by a liquorice-coloured cable. 'I knew we had this somewhere,' said Dad, flipping out the monitor and coaxing the ancient looking video camera back to life. 'It was in the garage under all my old skiing equipment.'

'What was it doing in the garage?'

'Mum asked me to chuck it away the first time she got sick. She didn't want anyone filming her until she was . . . until she was better. We only used it the once.'

I couldn't believe what he'd just said. He occasionally referred to her as 'your mother' or 'Jilly' even, but he hadn't called her plain 'Mum' like that for as long as I could remember. 'What's on it, Dad?'

'You'll have to wait and see,' he said, pressing the *Play* button and joining me on the sofa.

The sound was a bit scratchy, but it was definitely Dad behind the camera. He was doing his impression of that wildlife guy, whispering a commentary as he pushed open the kitchen door and walked out to the garden.

'And here in deepest England we see the female of the species, basking in the glorious August sunshine.'

There was a stripy deckchair in the middle of the lawn. All you could see of the person lounging in it was a tantalising glimpse of blond highlights.

'The survival instinct in these creatures is extraordinary. Notice the generous glass of chilled Sauvignon and the paperback book in her hand.'

All I wanted was for her to turn around.

Dad's accent changed to phoney American. 'Are you ready for your close up, Mrs Bridges?'

'Get that thing away from me,' she said, hiding her face behind *The Time Traveler's Wife*.

It was a heart stopping moment. The book came down and there was Mum, filling the screen with a smile so unforgettable it was hard to believe that I'd almost forgotten it.

A second later she was gone. The picture panned to a small girl in a purple swimsuit racing towards the camera pursued by a rotund Spiderman. Armed to the teeth, the six-year-old assassins set about their – surprisingly tolerant – victims with a volley of wet sponges and a pump-action water pistol.

The TV screen went spotty for a moment. And suddenly we were in the kitchen. Spiderman and the girl in the swimming costume (I loved that costume, it had mermaids all over it) were sitting at a red plastic table eating cupcakes. And if Spiderman's mystery identity was ever in doubt, he blew it completely by pulling his mouth hole wider so he could cram more cake in. Grunt never could resist Mum's cooking.

I've played it hundreds of times since then, and the last bit's definitely the best. Unbeknown to Mum, the camera cuts away from the young diners and up to her face. That's where it stays for the next twenty seconds. Only for some reason (I like to think it's because she's so happy) Mum doesn't notice she's being filmed. It's a special moment because the camera loves her, and so does the cameraman, and so does the small girl in the purple swimsuit.

But suddenly Mum realises what's happening and flashes her palm at the camera. 'Turn it o—'

And the screen goes blank.

'That's it, I'm afraid,' said Dad, jumping up to turn off the telly and dabbing his eyes with his shirtsleeve when he thought I couldn't see.

'Why have you never shown me this before?'

'I don't know really. I think I was afraid I'd miss her even more. Funny thing is, it was actually really lovely to see her moving like that.'

'So why now?'

'It's what you said at half term, I suppose. She's part of you, isn't she? I know how hard it's been, Beth, growing up without your mum. The least I can do is tell you everything I know about her.'

If you listened to Mrs Woolf's English lessons, you'd probably get the impression that human existence was a never-ending succession of ironies. And here was another one. Hannah's own life was a complete mess, but she'd still managed to give me some pretty good advice about Dad.

A smile can tell you everything. There was about a million miles between Mum's contented expression in the video and the feeble parody of happiness waiting for me in my bedroom.

Hannah had sent me a message at last. Well, not a message exactly, a photograph; a simple selfie, with a swirl of graffiti in the background, that was obviously designed to put my mind at rest.

The fact that she'd shaved her hair was a clue in itself,

but it was the smile that gave the game away. Teeth bared, like a frightened monkey, her eyes drowning in despair. It was a big fat fake of a smile that didn't fool me for a minute.

That's when I knew I'd have to tell someone. No, not just 'someone', someone special, someone who wouldn't start judging me – the one person in the world I could totally trust.

Dad was still fiddling with the camera as I slipped my phone into my coat pocket, pushed open the back door and disappeared into the night.

ACT FIVE

ACT FIVE

48
Hours

'Is George in?'

It was Friday night. Where else would he be?

Grunt's mum eyed me suspiciously. 'Hello Beth. Long time no see.'

'Yes, I've been . . .'

'So I hear,' said Mrs Grant, dipping a chocolate finger into a huge mug of tea.

'Can I see him then?'

I'd known Karen Grant since I was four years old. This was the first time she hadn't greeted me with a life-threatening hug. 'I'm sorry, Beth. I'm not sure he wants to see you.'

'Please. It's really important. There's something I need to tell him.'

Like the chocolate finger, she was already starting to

melt. 'It's cold out there, Bethy. You'd better come in.'

The rest of Grunt's family were in the lounge watching *Malcolm in the Middle*. I glimpsed them through the open door: his three siblings lined up on the sofa, Phil Grant tucked up beneath the newspaper in his favourite chair.

It was Sophie, the eight-year-old, who spotted me first. 'Hi Beth,' she called. 'Want to play *Animal Crossing*?'

'Sorry Soph, not tonight. I've got to see George about something.'

Grunt's younger brothers yelled out inappropriate suggestions.

'He's in his room,' said Mrs Grant, waving her (chocolate) finger at Billy and Nat. 'But, Beth?'

'Yes.'

'Tread a bit carefully, eh? I don't know what you said to him, but he's not been himself lately.'

'Yeah, course,' I said, anxiety mounting as I climbed the stairs and headed for the door with the *Already Disturbed* sticker on the front.

I knocked twice.

No answer.

I knocked again.

Still no answer.

I knocked louder and shouted, 'It's me – Beth. Can I come in?'

This time I didn't wait for an answer. I'd always avoided Grunt's bedroom. Not because I felt threatened, but because it was a health hazard. The mountain of dirty clothes behind the door turned opening it into a trial of strength, and a survival expert could have lasted weeks on the dying crisp packets.

He didn't notice me at first. For someone who hadn't been himself lately, Grunt looked surprisingly Grunt-like. 'Alluringly' dressed in only a hoodie and some boxer shorts, he was sitting at his little white desk, gazing lovingly into his laptop, a family pack of Snickers at his side.

'Bloody hell,' he said, jumping to his feet and covering his boxers with the nearest available album cover. 'What are *you* doing here?'

'What do you think?'

'You said you never wanted to see me again.'

'Yeah, I know, I'm really sorry about that,' I said, taking a peak at the craggy coastline on his laptop.

'It's only a game,' he protested. 'It's nothing . . . you know.'

According to Grunt, *Dear Esther* was the twenty-first-century equivalent of the novel. It looked more like wandering aimlessly around a remote Hebridean island to me.

'Sit down,' he said, clearing a space for me on the bed. 'I'll just get changed.'

'Thanks.'

Two minutes later he was back at his desk, having slipped into something more comfortable: the Spiderman dressing gown he'd paid thirty-nine dollars for (plus postage and packing) on eBay. 'Come to think of it, why should I talk to you anyway?'

'Because you're the only person I can trust.'

His Spidey sense was obviously tingling. 'It's about Hannah Taylor, isn't it?'

'Why do you say that?'

'Because it always is,' he said, turning back to his laptop. 'Have they found them or something?'

'No.'

A moody cello rose above the ambient wailing. Grunt stroked his mouse-pad. 'Maybe they've had face transplants.'

'Look, it's not funny, okay?'

'That's not what everyone at school's saying.'

'Yeah, well that lot are idiots. They don't realise how much it's hurting Hannah.'

He glanced up from his laptop. 'What?'

'I mean, well, she's bound to have seen some of the stuff on telly. I expect she's checked Facebook too. She's . . . probably in a right state.'

We'd been friends for too long. His Spidey sense was positively prickling. 'You know something, don't you?'

I nodded.

'Okay, Beth, start talking.'

So I did, starting with the kiss in Mr Moore's office right through to the stolen mobile and Hannah's tearful message.

By the time I'd finished, Grunt had lost all interest in the deserted farmhouse. 'You have to tell someone about this.'

'I just did, didn't I?'

For the first time ever, it was Grunt who sounded like the adult. 'Listen Beth, you can't keep her stupid secrets forever.'

'She trusts me. I'm not going to bail on her now.' It was all becoming clearer. 'No, what I've got to do is persuade her to come home.'

Grunt snorted. 'Why are you so bothered about her anyway? She deserves everything she gets for doing a runner with Martin Scorsese.'

'She says she loves him.'

Grunt thought for a moment. 'Yeah . . . well . . . anyone can fall for the wrong person, I suppose. But that's not the point. How can you persuade her to come home? She's not even answering your calls.'

'Because she can't,' I said. 'If he finds out she's carrying a phone, he'll force her to dump it.'

'So what are you going to do?'

'I'll have to go and find her, won't I?'

'Yeah, right,' said Grunt, spraying the screen with a film of partially digested Snickers. 'You don't know where she is – *do you*?'

'Listen to this,' I said, taking out my phone. 'It's the message she left two days ago.'

'*. . . If I can't be with him, I think I'd rather . . . Look, if anything happens to me, tell Mum I . . .*'

By the end, Grunt's default, ironic smirk had turned into something suspiciously sympathetic. 'Mnnn, yeah, you're right. She does sound pretty grim.' The smirk returned. 'Mind you, who wouldn't sound grim after "sharing a hotel room" with that loser?'

I slid up the bed towards him. 'I thought the background noises might be a clue. Couldn't you analyse them or something?'

'I may look like James Bond,' said Grunt, 'but I'm not a miracle worker. Sorry, Beth, unless you could hear Big Ben or something it really won't help.'

'We've got to do something. The longer this goes on, the worse she'll get. You heard what that psychiatrist woman said.'

'What psychiatrist woman?'

'Doesn't matter. There's got to be another way. She looked like death in that photo.'

'Photo?' said Grunt, suddenly looking interested again. 'You didn't tell me you had a photo.'

'She only just sent it. Believe it or not it was supposed to put my mind at rest. Don't worry – it's not got the Taj Mahal in the background. It could be anywhere.'

'Let's have a look.'

I showed him my phone. 'See what I mean? She looks terrible, doesn't she?'

Grunt was already tapping at his keyboard. 'It depends what kind of mobile she sent it from. But if the GPS is activated then it's probably Geotagged.'

'Geo what-ed?'

'Give it here. I'll email it to myself.' A moment later, it arrived in his inbox. 'Right, now all I need is an EXIF viewer.' A few more clicks and Spider-Man was sounding very pleased with himself. 'She took it this afternoon, at two thirty-seven and eight seconds. If you ask me, it's almost like she *wanted* to be found.'

'Where is she?'

'Let's just click on Google maps and find out, shall we?' He stared into his laptop. 'You're not going to believe this.'

'What?'

'She's in France.'

'You're joking.'

'I wish I was,' said Grunt.

'Are you sure?'

'Positive,' said Grunt. 'She's right *there* – Rue Joséphin Soulary.'

'And where's that?'

'It's in Lyon,' he said, switching to street view. 'Now here's the clever part. See that wall there, with the black graffiti? I reckon that's exactly where she took the photograph.'

I wouldn't say I could have kissed him, but a lifetime's supply of his confectionary of choice was a definite possibility. 'Then that's where I have to go.'

'You're not serious about that, are you? It's a bit more than a bus ride, Beth.'

'I can afford it. There's plenty of money in my bank account.'

'And what about Mr Moore? He's not exactly going to stand there while you talk her into coming home.'

'I'm not scared of him. Look, I have to do this, it's the only way.'

Grunt reached for a calming Snickers. 'Yes, but why? I don't get it.'

'*Because*,' I said, not really knowing how to explain. In spite of everything, the short time I'd spent with Hannah Taylor still felt really special. She'd given me a glimpse of the person I could become. 'Because she's my friend,' I said.

'All she's ever done is lie to you,' said Grunt. 'Funny kind of friend, if you ask me.'

'Look, she needs my help, okay?'

'Call the police. Like any other sane person.'

'I can't,' I said, certain now that I was doing the right thing. 'If she thinks they're closing in on her, she could easily panic. You said yourself she sounded terrible. Who knows what she might do? That's why I need to get to her first.'

'It'll take forever on the train,' said Grunt. 'By the time you get there they could be miles away.'

'Then I'll have to fly. That way I can get there and back on the same day.'

Grunt looked seriously gobsmacked. My fear of flying was one of his favourite comedy routines. 'You're really going to do this, aren't you?'

'Yes.'

'And how about your dad? What are you going to tell him?'

'He's off first thing tomorrow. He doesn't even need to know.'

Grunt shook his head. 'This is *such* a bad idea, Beth.'

'But you'd do the same for me, right?'

He didn't even have to think about it. 'Yeah.'

'Well then.'

'I really ought to tell someone about this.'

'You won't though, will you?'

It was almost like he was trying to talk himself into it. 'Well at least you know the language, I suppose. But you have to phone me the moment you get there. And keep in touch the whole time.'

'Yeah, course.'

And suddenly he was tapping at his keyboard again. 'What are you doing?'

'Booking your flight; you wouldn't have a clue, would you? Now, you'll need to leave as early as possible. What time's your dad going?'

'Hang on a minute. There's just one problem. I don't have my debit card.'

'That's okay,' said Grunt with a guilty smile. 'I know your number anyway.'

About an hour and two technical hitches later, Grunt came back from the wireless printer on the landing with my travel details. 'You'll need the 6.23 train to Gatwick because your flight leaves at 8.15. When you arrive at Lyon Airport you have to take the rhônexpress to the city centre. There's five Euros for a one-day pass on the Métro; the machines only take coins. Call me when you get to Croix-Rousse station and I'll talk you through the last part. And don't forget your passport – I know what you're like.'

He handed me my boarding pass.

'Okay, Beth, you've got forty-eight hours. Well, not really – more like four-and-a-half by the time you get there. But I've always wanted to say that.'

Taking
Off

This time the sick bag wasn't metaphorical. It was balanced on my lap throughout the cabin crew's dumb show. And I was pretty sure I'd soon be needing it when the seat-belt lights lit up and we taxied towards the runway.

Dad had talked me through it a thousand times, but I was still terrified. I was terrified of the ding-dong noises and the hum of the air-conditioning, I was terrified when I glanced out at the wing wobbling in the wind, and my heart was positively palpitating as the engines roared, forcing me back into my seat, and the huge metal bird thrust its beak into the sky.

But I'll tell you what terrified me more than anything: the nagging feeling that I'd left it too late.

Waiting for Hannah
(Part Two)

Grunt had briefed me – at length – on the weather. I was glad now I'd taken his advice and opted for at least five layers, because the icy blast that froze my features as I emerged from the Métro nearly took my breath away.

'How was your flight?'

'I don't want to talk about it.'

'The best metaphors are taken, eh?'

'Try being buried alive in a mile-high metal box plus all my worst Christmases rolled into one.'

'Well at least you made it; that's the main thing.'

I'd never felt so relieved to hear Grunt's voice. He was sitting in front of Google maps waiting to talk me down.

'Okay, so you're standing in the Place de la Croix-

Rousse. Look to your left and you should see a statue of a . . . *Shhhhhhhhhhhhhhhhhhhhhhhhhhhhhhhhh* . . .'

'You're dropping out, I can't —'

'I said you should see a statue of a woman scratching her arm.'

'Yep, got it. But I don't think she's scratching her —'

'Doesn't matter. Head towards the post office on the other side of the square and start walking down the hill.'

It was like an extreme version of that trust game where you directed a blindfolded partner round the drama studio. As the streets got meaner and narrower, there was no one I would have trusted more as my guide.

'Nearly there now, Beth. Turn left into Rue Belfort. There's a yellow shop on the corner called *Plomberie Chauffage* . . . What's so funny?'

'Your terrible French,' I said. 'Did you actually listen to anything Miss Bruni said?'

'Can you see it or not?'

'I see it, I see it.'

'Okay, keep going. There should be a restaurant on your right.'

'*Le Comptoir du Vin?*'

'Check. Now, a bit further down you'll come to some kind of church. Cross the road. There's an internet café on the corner.'

'I can see the café, but I can't see the church.'

'It's right in front of you,' said Grunt. '*Chapellerie*; it

203

says so on the window.'

'That's a hat shop, you idiot.'

It was the first time I'd heard him laughing since the farting horse video. 'At least I got you there in one piece.'

'What?'

'You've arrived, Beth. Rue Joséphin Soulary. Cross the road and you're there.'

He was right. Flanked on both sides by five-storey apartment buildings, it felt deserted after the shop-filled streets.

'Found the exact spot yet?' said Grunt.

'Yes, it's right here,' I said, studying the swirl of graffiti where Hannah had snapped that dismal self-portrait.

'Good luck, Beth. Call me again in an hour.'

I started full of optimism, tramping the freezing streets around Rue Joséphin Soulary for several hours before reality started to intervene. After all, they were in hiding. It wasn't as if they'd be walking round arm in arm like a honeymoon couple.

Mr Catchpole would probably have had a heart attack, but eventually I started approaching total strangers, showing them Hannah's photo and enquiring, '*Pardon, avez-vous vu ma copine?*'

The man in the hat shop promised to look out for her, several people said how pretty she looked, and I even had a compliment about my French. It was only the guy in the café where I stopped for an emergency pee break who had a feeling he might *just* have seen Hannah.

Every time I called Grunt, I sounded more despondent; every time he encouraged me to take a rest, I told him I was fine and started walking again.

But by four o'clock, I was all walked out. The internet café on the corner fitted my mood perfectly. With a couple of middle-aged men reviewing their on-line dating prospects and a Japanese student checking Facebook, it reeked of desperation. But it was a good place to keep watch, so I paid the guy with the white bushy eyebrows for half an hour and took my place at the workstation by the window.

For a while I scanned the street outside and pretended to watch YouTube. After one talking goat too many, I felt so sorry for myself that I Skyped Grunt.

'You should be heading back to the airport soon,' he said. 'Just call the police. It's one-one-two from a mobile.'

'I can't, not yet. She's round here somewhere, I know she is.'

'You've done your best, Beth. What more can you do?'

'I don't know, but I have to find her.'

'You look freezing,' he said, offering me a steaming David Bowie mug of hot chocolate. 'Why don't you call it a day?'

'Ten more minutes.'

He moved closer to the camera, dropping his voice on the way. 'This probably isn't a good time, but I was thinking, Beth . . . maybe when you get back we could go see a —'

'Oh my God, I don't . . .' A vision in black had flashed past the window. 'Sorry got to go. I think I just saw . . .' I grabbed my bag, called 'Catch you later' at the mystified face on the computer screen and raced outside to follow my vision.

I wasn't sure at first. I suppose I'd expected to see them together. It was the hunched shoulders and DJ headphones that gave him away. He was hurrying along Rue Joséphin Soulary with a baguette under his arm. Halfway down, he stopped in a doorway and whispered at the entry phone.

'Wait,' I shouted.

The door clicked, he pushed it open.

It was a weird time for me to be thinking about etiquette. But although he'd told us to call him Steve when we were out of school, I still couldn't bring myself to do it. 'Mr Moore . . . wait!'

This time he heard me, wrenching off his headphones and turning like a cornered rat. I was obviously the last person he'd expected. 'What are *you* doing here?'

'I've come to find Hannah.'

It was a weird time for *him* to be thinking like a teacher. 'You came all this way on your own? You do realise how dangerous that is?'

'Look you're not my teacher now, okay? And you never will be.'

The untamed stubble made him look much older.

'You think I don't know that?'

'So where is she then?'

'Boys Don't Cry' was still jangling on his shoulders. 'We can't talk here,' he said, checking the pavement opposite before waving me into a dank corridor with a trio of wheelie bins in the corner.

Once inside, he was a lot less friendly. 'Why do you want to see Hannah?'

'I'm her friend.'

'Are you sure about that, Beth?'

'What do you mean?'

His eyes flamed in the darkness. 'The friendship thing was my idea. I had a feeling you were onto us, so I told her to keep an eye on you.'

Even if it wasn't the shock of the century, it still hurt like hell. 'Maybe that's how it started, but it's not like that any more. Hannah needs me, I know she does.'

I thought I knew him, but he was starting to scare me. 'If you were any kind of friend, you'd leave her alone. I told her we were settled here. But we can't stay now.'

'Where is she anyway?'

'Upstairs. We're renting a flat.'

'I want to see her,' I said, trying to sound forceful, but not succeeding.

'Well she doesn't want to see you.'

'Yes she does. She's in a terrible state.'

'She's fine,' said Mr Moore, finally silencing his iPod. 'In fact, she's holding it together better than I am.'

'Well, she looks terrible.'

'What do you mean?' All of a sudden he didn't sound so confident. 'How would you know what she looks like?'

'She sent me a photo.'

'How could she? She hasn't got a phone.'

'Maybe you don't know her as well as you think.'

'Stupid,' he said, stabbing the air with his baguette. 'I told her about that. Why does she never listen?'

The lid that I'd been keeping on my anger suddenly flew off. 'Do you even care about Hannah? She's hundreds of miles from home. It probably feels like the whole world's against her. And you won't even let her phone a friend.'

'I love her, Beth,' he said simply. 'Do you honestly think I'd have given up everything, if I just didn't care?'

'I know that's what you want me to think. But she's just a schoolkid. You should be ashamed of yourself.'

'You can't help who you fall in love with, Beth.'

'You were her teacher. It's your job to help it.'

'So now you're going to make things worse, are you; forcing her to run again?'

'Tell you what,' I said, thinking on my feet for once. 'I'll do you a deal. You can go. I won't say anything, promise. But leave Hannah. I'll tell her you decided to do the right thing.'

'Right for who?' he said. 'I'm not making any deals with you. She's fine. She's happy. We just want to be together.'

'If she's so happy, why did she sound like this?' I took out my phone and played him Hannah's message.

And after it was over, he found it hard to speak. 'Yeah, well, that doesn't mean . . .' He tapped his foot on the hard stone floor. 'Sure, she's a bit . . . anxious . . . but . . . basically she's fine.'

'I want to hear Hannah say that.'

'All right,' he said, sliding open the lift door and stepping inside. 'Follow me.' A month ago I'd have given anything to be caged up with Mr Moore like that. But I could barely look at him as we shuddered up to the fourth floor.

The tiny flat was cold and bare; just a bed in the middle, a few bits of furniture and a microwave.

There was already a hint of sadness in Hannah's voice. 'I'm in the loo, babe. How did the interview go?'

'You'd better get your stuff together,' said Mr Moore. 'We've got to get out of here.'

The hint of melancholy became full blown despair. 'You're joking. Why? You said it was safe here.'

'Friend to see you,' said Mr Moore.

Her savagely cropped hair looked far worse in real life. But at least she seemed happy to see me, clambering across the bed and giving me a real Year Nine hug. 'Beth, how did you find us?'

'That photo you sent.'

'Sorry Steve,' she said meekly. 'I didn't think.'

'Why would you do that, Hannah?' said Mr Moore, sounding more like a teacher than he'd ever done at school. 'I've told you a thousand times.'

'I don't know,' she said, tears already tumbling. 'I just wanted to talk to someone.'

'If you want to talk to someone, you talk to me,' said Mr Moore. 'How often do I have to say it, Hannah, we can't trust anyone.'

'Well I trust Beth,' she said. 'And I keep thinking I might never see her again.'

'Of course you'll see her again,' said Mr Moore. 'In a few years' time, it'll be safe to go back.'

'Yeah, I know that,' said Hannah. 'It just seems such a long —'

I figured it was my last chance. There was no point in holding back. 'You've got to come home, Hannah. You can't stay with him.'

Hannah looked mystified. 'What are you talking about? I love him. What else would I do?'

'Well he doesn't love you, not really. Otherwise he wouldn't be putting you through all this.'

'It's what I want,' said Hannah.

There was no stopping me now. 'No you don't. I can tell from your messages. You're in so deep you don't know how to get out.'

'Stop putting words into her mouth,' said Mr Moore.

'Why?' I said. 'That's exactly what you've been doing.'

Hannah's howl of pain was heartbreaking. 'Stop it, please, I don't think I can . . .'

Mr Moore glared accusingly. 'Now look what you've done.'

I glared back. 'You've got to come home, Hannah. Your family needs you.'

'Steve needs me more,' she said. 'I'm not leaving him, Beth.'

There had been a time when his smile seemed so captivating. Right now it looked unbelievably smug. 'You heard her. She's not going anywhere.'

'You can't keep running forever,' I said. 'Your photos are everywhere. It's all over the internet. They'll track you down in the end, Hannah. If I can find you, they will too.'

'Don't listen to her,' said Mr Moore. 'If we stick to the plan we'll be fine.'

It was certainly a long shot, but it was worth a try. 'Okay then, if Hannah won't leave you, you'll have to take her home yourself. Do the right thing for once.'

His laugh was as hollow as an Easter egg. 'Are you kidding? I know exactly what everyone thinks of me. I wouldn't last five minutes.'

What else could I say? Hannah's mind was obviously made up. There was no way I could change it for her. 'So you're really . . . sure about this, are you?'

'Yes,' she whispered.

'You heard her,' said Mr Moore. 'Now please, just leave us alone. She's upset enough as it is.'

'All right, but I need to say goodbye first.'

Hannah took me by the hands, squeezing like she never wanted to let go. 'You're a good friend, Beth. I just wish we'd had more time together. Maybe in a few years we can . . .' Our tears could have filled a reservoir. 'I'll see you when I see you, yeah?'

'Sure.'

'Oh and Beth?'

'Yes.'

'Promise me you won't tell anyone.'

'I promise,' I said.

Mr Moore grabbed her arm, pulling her away from me and wrapping his arm around her, like a jealous boyfriend. 'Take care, Beth.'

'I'll be off then,' I said, taking one last look around their dismal flat. 'And good luck. I think you're going to need it.'

It was the hardest decision I'd ever made.

But I knew it was the right one. Hannah hadn't kept her promises, so why should I keep mine? The moment I stepped out of the lift, I reached for my phone. '*Allo, police? Je pense que j'ai des informations concernant l'écolière anglaise qui a disparue.*'

Five minutes later, they were hammering on the door. And I watched from the other side of the road as they bundled them into separate police cars; Mr Moore white with fury, Hannah wailing hysterically that she'd love him forever.

Epilogue

Miss Carver said she liked my movie script. *Trust Games* was 'well constructed, with largely believable characters and some snappy dialogue', but someone on the senior management team felt the subject matter wasn't quite appropriate for GCSE coursework, so she encouraged me to submit a piece about internet pornography instead.

I'd changed the names of course, and the Grunt character was a wisecracking Polish girl, but most of it was pretty much how it actually happened. It was only the final scene, where the two girls meet in the Learning Resources Centre, that I rewrote completely. 'Helen' thanks 'Liz' for coming to Berlin to find her. She's already regretting the unhealthy relationship with 'Mr Morgan' and in the very last shot Liz and Helen are seen walking arm in arm towards the canteen.

But it didn't happen like that.

We all saw the picture of Mr Moore in handcuffs. In fact, it lasted almost twenty minutes on the Year Eleven notice board with the caption *You're Going Down!* underneath. And for a while they still made the headlines. Hannah's photo was everywhere. There was even a story (probably not true) about her being signed up by a top modelling agency. But a couple of corrupt MPs and a juicy celebrity scandal later, Steve and Hannah were just random names and not a subject that practically everyone in the country had an opinion on.

Three weeks into the summer term, Hannah eventually turned up in school. Her hair was growing back, but she still looked a ghost of her former self. Rumour had it she was seeing a counsellor, although nobody really knew because she hardly ever talked to anyone.

I was desperate to make contact again. Perhaps she'd forgiven me at last. But when we did finally come within spitting distance – a chance meeting in the reception block toilets – Hannah looked like she wanted to do just that.

'Why couldn't you leave us alone?' she said, fixing me in the mirror as she washed her hands of me. 'You had to stick your nose in, didn't you? Well do me a favour, yeah? Keep away from me. I never want to see your self-righteous little face again. You've ruined my life and I hate you for it.'

Ironically, it was thanks to Hannah that *my* life was looking so good again. She'd given me the courage to make new friends, not to mention value my oldest one. And Dad and I were really talking at last. In fact, now that I seemed to have conquered my fear of flying, we were even considering visiting Mum's favourite art gallery in Venice. Hannah would always be a huge part of me, but little by little I was putting the past behind me and learning to focus on the future.

And that's how I hoped it would be for Hannah; that in the end she'd start forgetting; that she'd stop being 'the girl who ran off with the teacher' and become just Hannah again. She might even come to realise that what Mr Moore did was wrong. And hopefully, one day soon, she'll find something better to feel passionate about: acting perhaps – she was brilliant at that. Like Dave Denyer said, it was a real tragedy that no one got to see her Juliet.

The last time I saw Hannah was at the school prom. Why she went in the first place, I can't begin to imagine. But that didn't excuse what they did to her – especially the cardboard cut-out of Mr Moore. And if I hadn't been outside, paying a courtesy visit to Grunt's 'vintage' ice-cream van, I would have done everything in my power to stop them. Unfortunately, that could be the least of her worries. Because as she raced across the car park in her strappy red prom dress, I'm almost certain I spotted a tiny bump.

THE BEX FACTOR

When Bex gets an audition for *The Tingle Factor*, she begs geeky guitarist Matthew to accompany her – but the judges want Matthew – not Bex!

Bex swallows her envy, and persuades a reluctant Matthew to take part by offering to help with his family. While Matthew gets swept up in the world of reality TV, it's Bex who has to deal with his sweet, affection-starved sister and his angry, disabled mother.

COMING TO GET YOU

Sam Tennant has been brutally murdered in an online computer game. What's worse, it looks like his killers are out to get him in real life too.

'The Emperor' and 'Ollyg78' say they know him from school. Soon they turn his classmates against him too, and Sam's only support comes from terminally shy Abby and Stephen the class nerd. As the threats become more sinister, Sam faces a desperate struggle to identify his persecutors before things really get deadly.

An absorbing, fast-paced thriller.

FiREWaLLeRS

Jess returns from a nightmare day at school to find her dad's been suspended from work and gone into hiding.

To escape the slobbering newshounds all eager for the full story, Mum drags Jess and her sister off to a remote Scottish island. Modern technology's forbidden, and there's only a bunch of teenage über geeks for company.

Without Facebook or even her mobile, Jess feels totally disconnected from everybody back home.

And why are they there anyway?

What are they really running away from?

SILENCED

At first I thought there were technical problems – something wrong with the sound system – because when I opened my mouth I couldn't hear a thing. But it was more serious than that . . . I was completely dumb.

Chris loses the power of speech completely when his best friend dies in a car crash.

But why? What terrible secret is he hiding?

And can he find his voice before it's too late?

A powerful, original, thought-provoking thriller.

Piccadilly

piccadillypress.co.uk/teen

Go online to discover:

☆ more books you'll love

☆ competitions

☆ sneak peeks inside books

☆ fun activities and downloads

Find us on Facebook and Twitter for
exclusive competitions, giveaways and more!

www.facebook.com/piccadillypressbooks

www.twitter.com/PiccadillyPress